WYOMING GUN LAW

LEE FLOREN

Thorndike Press • Thorndike, Maine

Thorndike Large Print ® Popular Series edition
published in 1993 by arrangement with Dorchester
Publishing Co., Inc., New York City.

The tree indicium is a trademark of Thorndike Press.

Set in 16 pt. News Plantin by Juanita Macdonald.

This book is printed on acid-free, high opacity paper. ∞

Library of Congress Cataloging in Publication Data

Floren, Lee
    Wyoming gun law / Lee Floren.
      p. cm.
    ISBN 1-56054-640-9 (alk. paper : lg. print)
    1. Large type books. I. Title.
    [PS3511.L697W96 1993]
    813'.54—dc20
                                       92-43521
                                          CIP

WYOMING GUN LAW

ONE

The Cheyennes say that when a great man dies a shooting star streaks across the black Wyoming night. But no shooting star soared across the sky the night that Big Bob Williams died in the immense ranch house he had built on Ringbone Creek — the home ranch of his mighty Cross in the Circle.

And Big Bob was a great man.

When only twenty he had trailed wild longhorns north into Wyoming Territory. Now he was seventy-three . . . and he was dying. He had worn out three wives. Two had been barren but the third had produced him a son.

Sometimes, in bitter anger, he had cursed the day that son, Matt Williams, had been born.

He knew he was dying.

That thought held no fear. Pain had long fallen back before the pressure of Death. Therefore he had no pain. He lay with his once powerful body shrunken and thin.

He had no eyes for his son who stood beside the bed.

Matt Williams looked at the Crow squaw who held Big Bob's bony hand as it dangled over the side of the bed.

"How does he feel, Many Feathers?"

The Crow squaw looked up, her eyes shiny beads, and she shook her dark big head. Matt put his hand, palm down, on the old cowman's chest.

He felt the heart push pressure against his palm. Big Bob opened his eyes slowly.

"Matt?"

"Yes, Big Bob."

He had never been *son* to Big Bob. Nor had he ever called his sire anything but Big Bob. Never dad or father. Never son or boy.

That explained their feelings to each other.

"Matt, the days of open range are over with," the dying man said.

"I don't agree with you, Big Bob."

The eyes swept across him, then closed. The squaw watched and her face was dark and impassive. She had been Big Bob's fourth "wife". In those days a white man did not marry a squaw. She just became his wife without religious or civil ceremony.

"Don't start a range war, son."

Matt Williams' craggy face showed a frown. Never before, in his memory, had his sire called him "son".

"I'll not have squatters on Cross in a Circle range," Matt said.

The white lips moved. "Not our range. They take up the land legally. Our day — the day of open range — is gone. . . ."

Dark anger swept across Matt Williams' face. He was twenty-eight, and he had never married but he had had his share of women, both redskins and white. He was six-feet one, straight as a Crow buck, but the gods had cursed him the day he had been born, and the gods had given him ambition. Big Bob had said this ambition would destroy his son. He had told Many Feathers that and both had wondered about the future.

"I don't agree."

Big Bob lay silent, face ashen.

Many Feathers said, "You go, please, Matt."

Anger grooving his face, Matt Williams turned and walked out on the porch. He stood there and looked at the sky. There were millions of stars up there. And he remembered the old Cheyenne legend.

Odd, the older a person got, the more he swung back to his childhood beliefs. Matt Williams looked at the stars and waited . . . and impatience was raw in him. Why didn't the Old Man die and get it over with?

An owl hooted in the willows along the creek and a trout splashed there as he leapt after a night insect. The earth was damp and good, for a rain had fallen the day before, and he got the smell of the earth — the smell of green bluestem grass, of flowering sagebrush, of willows and cottonwoods. A man should not die on a night this peaceful. But still, Big Bob was dying.

A man came out of the night. He sighed and sat on the steps, and he looked up at Matt Williams. This man had very heavy shoulders, he was not over five-four in height, and his thighs were like thick boles of a pine tree.

"How is he, Matt?"

"Dying, Keller."

Ag Keller rolled a cigarette with huge fingers — but fingers singularly fast near any gun. "To every man upon this earth, death cometh soon or late," he quoted.

"For hell's sake, quit that!"

Ag Keller lit the cigarette and the match showed his ugly, heavy face with the knife scar across the right jowl.

"Matt, don't jump on me."

"Then keep your mouth closed."

Keller sat silent, puffing his smoke. Lights from the bunkhouse threw rectangular layers across the Wyoming earth. A man came out of the barn, and entered the bunkhouse, the lighted doorway illuminating his gaunt height.

"The boys," said Keller, "are ready to ride, Matt." He flexed his gun-hand.

The squaw came out of the house, moving on padded moccasins, and she keened, "He is dead, he is dead!"

"When?" Matt Williams asked.

"Right now, he die."

Matt Williams pushed her hard, sending her against the wall. She seemed to break in two, and she sat down. "And no stars fell," Matt said. "Get your things, squaw, and be off this ranch before morning!"

"But your father said —"

"Big Bob is dead. Get off by morning."

Ag Keller stood up. "Shall I get the boys?"

"Get them! We ride."

"How many?"

"Three, besides us."

Matt Williams watched him go into the bunkhouse. Then the new owner of the big Cross in a Circle turned and looked down at the squaw. She was sobbing now. Her sobs were broken, low, and full of misery and pain.

Matt Williams kicked her. She sprawled across the porch, then got to her feet, cursed him, and ran into the house. He followed her.

11

She had taken a rifle off the deerhorns over the fireplace. He ripped the .30-30 from her hands. He did not know why he did not kill her. He hit her with the stock of the rifle across the back of the neck and knocked her unconscious.

He turned suddenly, as though expecting his father to come into the room, for his father, he knew, had loved this squaw more than any of his three wives. Then he remembered that Big Bob was dead, and that was good — for now he owned the Cross in a Circle.

Carrying the rifle, he went outside. Gravel crunched under his boots as he went toward the barn. A lantern hanging from the ridge beam showed the riders gathered there. Ag Keller held the reins of the big black four-year-old stallion.

"Saddled Midnight for you, Matt."

Matt Williams found a stirrup and lifted himself. "We got everything we need," Ag Keller said. "Powder to blow up hell, fire to start it burnin', and guns to notch off anybody."

"Where to, Matt?" a puncher asked.

Matt Williams said, "We raid that nester over on Lime Crick. He's single and we burn down his spread. We leave his carcass filled with lead as a warning to those others."

"We'll kill him," Ag Keller said.

Matt Williams turned the black. "Ride, men."

They roared out of the ranch's yard. Behind them the squaw lay on the floor, blood from her mouth; she breathed, but she was unconscious. In his bedroom Big Bob Williams lay with his mouth open, but no breath came from him.

Matt Williams looked at the sky.

"Not a star fell," he quoted himself.

Ag Keller leaned toward Matt. "You say something about *stars*, again, Matt?"

"Keep your damn mouth shut!" Matt Williams ordered.

TWO

The town of Ringbone, Territory of Wyoming, is situated on the flat, and the creek known as Ringbone Creek flows through it. When the railroad built into Ringbone in 1886, the town was then known as Williamstown, being named after Big Bob Williams, but the railroad changed the name to Ringbone, a fact that Big Bob had always resented.

Three days before the death of the cattle baron, a fat Mexican had ridden into Ringbone. He was a short, heavy-set man, almost as wide as he was tall, and he had a thick dark face, his jowls a little too heavy. He rode a horse with a Texas brand — a brand that came from the Panhandle country around what is now Lubbock, Texas. And a Texan who had, a few years before, come up the Trail with Cross in a Circle cattle, saw him and read the brand on the Mexican's bronc.

Accordingly, the Texan had swaggered out

of the Star Rowel Saloon and grabbed the reins of the Mexican's horse, forcing the animal to a halt.

"I used to work for the Mill Iron outfit on the Panhandle," the Texan declared. "Your hoss packs the Mill Iron brand. Them Mill Iron people don't sell their hosses to greasers, nor does a greaser work for them."

The implication was plain. The Texan was accusing the Mexican of stealing the Mill Iron horse.

"Me, I buy this horse," the Mexican said. "Now you take the hands off the reins, no?"

"You stole this Mill Iron bronc, eh?"

The Mexican showed a smile filled with white teeth. It was a disarming smile, yet the Texan was a little puzzled by the foolishness of the smile. Maybe the gent was *loco?*

"I got a beel-of-the-sale for thees bronc," the Mexican said. Grimy and stubby fingers dug into his vast pocket and came out with a folded square of dirty paper. The fingers straightened the paper and the Texan saw the thick lips purse.

"Thees ees not eet. Thees ees a letter from Conchita, my woman."

"You ain't got no bill-of-sale!"

"You call me the liar, no?"

"I say you lie!"

There was more to this than the discussion

15

about a horse. Texans hated Mexicans and the trailman was not interested in the horse's ownership — he wanted to kill a Mexican. The man, he knew, was about half drunk — his breath was vile with whiskey.

"I no lie!"

"I'm callin' you a liar, spic!"

The Texan had his right hand on his gun. The Mexican kicked him under the jaw. One moment the Mexican's right boot had been in the wide Sonora stirrup; the next, it was under the Texan's jaw — and it came in hard and fast.

The Mexican felt his boot-toe smash down the man's Adam's apple. He heard the crack of the Texan's jawbone. The Texan went back, his arms working, and he lifted his gun, swinging it as he fought for balance.

The Mexican was on his feet; the Texan felt the pistol being wrenched from his grip. Then he sat down and held his head and moaned, the fight and swagger gone out of him.

The town marshal — a man named Bill Jenkins — came running. The Mexican handed him the Texan's gun.

"He might get the hurt weeth the gon, Meester Marshal."

The marshal studied the Texan. He looked down at the man so he could hide the surprise

16

in his eyes. This did not seem possible.

"Who helped you down Sig Rudder, fellow?"

"Nobody he help me. I does eet all by my lonesome."

"He's a gunman," the marshal said. "He rides for the Cross in a Circle. That's a tough outfit. You've heard of it, I reckon?"

The Mexican had heard. But he said, "No, I stranger here. The name ees Tortilla Joe."

The Texan suddenly groaned and rolled over. In a thin, pained voice he said, "He busted my jaw. He kicked me in the face. My throat — I can't hardly speak. He took my gun."

A man came out of the Mercantile. Later the Mexican was to learn that this was Matt Williams. Williams said to the Texan, "Get on your lousy feet, Sig Rudder. Get over to the doctor's office. Get your jaw patched up."

Two townsmen helped Rudder up and took him down the street. Matt Williams looked at the Mexican. The man's eyes held a thoughtful scrutiny.

"I saw you down him, Mexican. You work fast and good."

"You hate him?"

"He worked for me," Williams said.

"You own Cross in Circle spread?"

"I do."

Williams got the impression that this man, who looked so lazy and soft and easy-going, was, in reality, a hell-cat in boots. There was something else in the Mexican's dove-like brown eyes. It was a silent and weighty appraisal. Matt Williams, for some reason, felt uneasy.

"I can use a man like you," Williams said.

"*Gracias,* but I no want job," Tortilla Joe said. "I hates the work. Work ees my enemy. I want to know where my enemies they are. One of my enemies ees then at the Cross een the Circle spread, no?"

Somebody laughed at the joke. Williams, though, did not laugh. Was it a joke? This Mexican said he had an enemy at the Cross in a Circle. Was that enemy labor — or was it a human enemy?

"That's one way to put it," Matt Williams said.

The Mexican said, "Me, I hears that the Cross een the Circle outerfit she ees owned by a mans named Beeg Bob Weeliams."

"He's my father. He's — sick."

"Oh, I sees."

Matt Williams said, "Mex, if I was you I believe I'd ride down the road talkin' to myself. You kicked around a Cross in a Circle rider. My 'outerfit' built this town and this country."

"I stay a few days?"

Matt Williams' eyes drew down. "Sig Rudder will be after you."

"Maybe then I works for you? You gives me a week or so to rest up?" The Mexican sighed with a great weariness. "I ride hard up the trails, mans."

Tortilla Joe wanted to give the impression that he was a wanted man, a *renegado*. Williams turned and then pivoted as a thought struck him, and this time his eyes were flint.

"Listen, mister, you ain't a nester, are you?"

"Me a farmer! You makes me laugh! Do the farmers bother you?"

"They've moved in," Williams said hurriedly. "My dad — he — Well, we'll run them out. They can't squat on Cross in a Circle grass and get away with it."

"You hire me as a gonman?"

"The same."

"Me, I theenks eet over."

"Don't think too long."

So Tortilla Joe stayed around Ringbone town. He drank a little — but not much; he found a woman who could make *tortillas* — she was the Mexican cook in the Spoon and Fork Café. Her name was Margarita and she had had five husbands and she wanted a sixth. Tortilla Joe saw desire in her dark eyes.

She smelled of garlic and peppers, though.

He had a bedroll and he slept out in the hills. Rudder got out of the *medico's* office and walked around town with his jaw wrapped up. His eyes were evil and small and scheming. The second night Tortilla Joe slept in the brush and he strung ropes around about ankle-high. Anybody who tried to sneak up on him in the dark would be tripped. Next morning he was back in Ringbone at the Spoon and Fork with Margarita fawning over him. She wore her dresses a little low in front and each time she had a chance she leaned over more than she should have leaned.

But who else could make such *tortillas?* The Mexican crunched through the crust and beans. Seasoned just right with chili peppers and salt. A good cook, but with five husbands behind her, how would the sixth fare?

"You are the nice womans."

"Me, I am not more than *nice,* Tortilla Joe?"

The Mexican realized he had said the wrong thing. He asked, "There ees a farmer here an' hees name ees Juan Powers?"

"*Si,* John Powers."

"Where ees hees farm?"

"The creek she ees called Hanging Woman's Creek. She ees northwest of town, on grass claimed by Big Bob Weeliams."

That night Sig Rudder jumped him. Tortilla Joe had to defend himself and when the roar ended Sig Rudder was dead. He was very, very dead. The top of his head was gone.

Sig Rudder had come out onto the plank sidewalk, and he had called Tortilla Joe all the dirty names he could remember. Tortilla Joe had tried to get away from him. He had had, finally, no other choice. Sig Rudder had a rep as a gunslinger. Yet, when it ended, he was dead; his bullet had gone low, and it had ripped into the plank sidewalk.

The marshal had said, "You can sure sling a sudden gun, Mexican. I saw Rudder jump you; it was self-defense in my book. But the book of Big Bob Williams is a different volume than mine. . . ."

"I do nothing against the Cross een a Circle."

"Why are you sticking around this burg?"

"Me, I likes the *senora* Margarita."

The marshal shook his head sadly. "I don't believe that, Tortilla Joe. You might like her *tortillas* but as for liking her . . . Don't say I didn't warn you, friend."

"*Gracias.*"

That night three things happened.

First, Big Bob Williams died in the big four-poster bed at the Cross in a Circle outfit, out on Ringbone Creek.

Big Bob had seen it was useless to fight the farmers. Now his hot-headed arrogant son,

Matt Williams, moved against the farmers right away.

Second, Matt Williams and his riders burned down the nester's spread on Lime Creek. They burned the man's shack to the ground, killed his livestock, and shot him and let him burn in his cabin.

The third thing was the arrival of one man — and that man was Tortilla Joe's partner, lanky Buck McKee.

THREE

They came riding through the starlight, hard-riding Wyoming men. They rode toward Buck McKee. And the lanky cowpuncher watched them streak down a hill about a quarter-mile ahead.

Buck McKee had a feeling, for some reason, that he was in danger. Men did not ride range in such a group unless they rode for deviltry. And Buck McKee knew there was trouble on this Ringbone range, for John Powers' letter had told him that.

He had intended to come quietly into Ringbone, scout around, and do some ground-work, but here these riders were bearing down on him. He counted five, and decided to beat a retreat. Accordingly he swung his bronc and started to lope away at an angle.

One of the riders hollered, "There rides a damned nester!" and Buck heard the whine of a bullet overhead. He saw the red flare of the man's pistol; another pistol cut the night with flame, too. By this time he was out of saddle, and on the ground, lying on his belly, his .45 across his forearm ahead of him.

Anger marked the cowpuncher's lank face. He knew nobody on this range except John Powers, and Powers was a friend — not an enemy. He shot once and he thought he saw a rider flinch in leather. Other riders shot, and then they thundered on into the night. Then there was the sound of their broncs' hoofs. And the faint lingering smell of Wyoming dust. . . .

Buck got to his feet. He was well over six feet tall, thin to a toothpick's gauntness, and he wore range-clothes. His hat lay about ten feet away and he walked over and retrieved it, and he still packed that puzzled scowl. The riders had shot at him, then had ridden on. . . . did this make sense?

Behind him was a steep hill, its surface marked by black igneous boulders. He saw now why they had not desired to wage a pitched battle. He could have retreated back into the boulders and there, with altitude on his side, he could have held off an army.

One had hollered, "There rides a damned nester!"

Evidently farmers were moving in on Ringbone.

He punched a new crease in his old hat and

restored it to his head and mounted. He would get out of here. He was sure he had wounded one of the night-riders. He remembered seeing the rider sag suddenly in saddle, as his bronc had continued running.

He was a little angry, too.

John Powers had written him, asking him to come for a visit. He and John had punched cows together up on the Milk River in Montana Territory. That had been almost ten years before.

These scissorbills — these night-riders — had had no reason or right to shoot at him. Who were they?

Somewhere ahead was Ringbone town. John Powers was there. John would answer his questions.

He rode to the crest of a low, rocky hill.

Even before he got to the top of the hill, he saw the red savage glare of the fire. Its flames marred the starlight of the Wyoming sky with an ugly smear of color. Then, as the top of the hill was gained, he saw about half a mile away a house was burning. Not much more than a shack; he could see the skeleton framework of it — the flames were eating up the studs and rafters with licking scarlet fingers.

Somewhere back in his mind he tied together two things — first, the night-riders;

second, this burning homestead shack. Evidently the cowpunchers he had run into were running a nester off of Ringbone range.

Perhaps some human down below needed his help. Perhaps somebody was wounded, or dying. . . . His spurs found his tired pony and lifted him to a lope toward the burning house.

He almost ran over the rider who came out of some high buckbrush. As it was, their broncs swerved, and Buck, surprised as he was, detected the glint of steel in the rider's hand.

His first thought was that the cowmen had left some riders behind to ambush any nesters who came to investigate the burning of the shack. He should have ridden around the burning shack, headed into Ringbone town and there reported the fire to the Law.

Just now, though, this rider had a pistol.

Buck McKee left his saddle. He moved with automatic easiness, and he got both arms around the rider's belt, and he dragged him to the ground. The pistol went off once. Because Buck had the rider's arms pinned, the bullet went straight down into the earth. The rider didn't shoot again. Buck got his thumb under the hammer of the .45.

The rider grunted something, and then they were rolling over; they rolled twice. When

26

they stopped Buck was on top, holding down the rider's arms. He panted, "What the hell you trying to do —", and then, suddenly, he stopped. He got to his feet. His face, for some reason, was flushed.

"So help me," he said huskily, "if it ain't *a woman!*" Her young face was struggling with uncontrollable anger. Quickly she got to her feet. She had lost her hat and dark hair tumbled around her small shoulders.

She slapped at him, saying angrily, "You big stupid ox! You could have killed me!"

Buck caught her wrist. He did not let go of it. She struggled, tried to slap him with her free hand; he got that, too.

She wore levis. Under her shirt her breasts rose and fell.

"Let go of me, you murdering Cross in a Circle killer!"

Buck said, "Don't push me too far, gal. I'll get mad and forget I'm a gentleman."

"You mean a killer, not a gentleman! Gentlemen don't draw wages from the Williams' spread!"

She kicked him on the shin.

Buck McKee said, "Ouch!" and released her hands. He sat on the ground and held his shin. "You got lead in the boot, Miss?"

She had her pistol. She held it in both hands. She pointed it at Buck who remained seated.

"I should kill you!"

Buck had a very uneasy moment. She was angry enough to pull the trigger. The heavy .45 wavered under her grip. Buck decided to do nothing. If he grabbed for the gun — then, sure as anything, she would shoot. She might hit him — and she might miss him. He decided to remain sitting down.

"What's this all about?" he wanted to know.

The flame of the burning cabin showed the tremor in her full lips. She had the clean, sweeping loveliness of open range, of sunshine. Their eyes met — hers angry and hot, his calm as he could make them.

Buck murmured, "Miss, I'm not a Cross in a Circle rider, as you said. I don't even know where that iron is *located*. You accused me of drawin' wages from the Williams' spread. Me, I don't know where that outfit is, so help me."

"Are you lying to me?"

"The last time I lied, Miss, my good old mother scrubbed my mouth with lye soap, and that broke me of lyin' forever."

"What are you doing here?"

He told her about meeting night-riders, how they had shot at him, and he told about seeing the fire and riding down to investigate.

"Then I ran into you and we have this ruckus."

She lowered the gun. She said, "I believe you, sir." She walked over and sat on a rock. "He's dead," she cried. "He's burning in his cabin."

"Who is he?"

"My neighbor. His name was Jack Maloney. He was an Irishman, and he always joked and laughed, but now he won't laugh again."

Buck was very solemn. "I'm a newcomer here, as I said. I take it there's a range-war here with this Williams' outfit trying to run out you farmers, and you are a farmer's wife?"

"I'm not married. Jack Maloney proposed to me — oh, many times — still, I liked him but didn't love him." She stopped suddenly. "I guess I'm a little stunned."

"Where do you live?"

Her name was Sandra Smith, and she and her father had a homestead about a mile away. Her father was named Pete Smith. He was in Ringbone town for supplies and would come back in the morning.

"Seems to me that other farmers would come to investigate the fire," he said.

"They're afraid to leave their homes. If they do the Cross in a Circle might burn them down while they were gone."

There was nothing Buck or anybody else could do here. He said he was heading into

Ringbone town and would report the fire to the sheriff. She told him Ringbone was not the county seat and therefore had no sheriff; not even a deputy.

"There's a town marshal — his name is Bill Jenkins — but his jurisdiction is just in Ringbone town and stops at the town's limits. The Williams' outfit wouldn't allow the sheriff to station a deputy in town. Evidently they want no interference from the law." She brushed dust from her levis and Buck noticed her full hips. "The marshal has his hands full in town. A stranger killed one of the Cross in a Circle gunmen. The man killed was named Rudder."

"A stranger killed him, you say? What is the stranger's name?"

"A Mexican called Tortilla Joe."

Buck nodded again. So Tortilla Joe, his old partner, had gunned down a Williams' rider. Buck then asked if she knew John Powers. Powers, she said, had a homestead on Hanging Woman's Creek.

"That dirty, stinking thief!"

"What's wrong with Powers?"

"Mister, you look like a pretty square-shooter to me. I'm sorry I tried to kill you, because any man who would ride down to see if anybody was caught in a fire is a good man in my book."

"Yes, Sandra."

"But, Mister, if you're a friend of that skunk John Powers, I want nothing to do with you, understand?"

"You make it clear. But why — ?"

Without answering, she mounted and rode away, dust rising behind her bronc as she loped towards her homestead.

Buck McKee scowled, then shook his head in puzzlement.

FOUR

The man lay in bed stark naked. His eyes were closed and his mouth was closed, too. His chest did not rise and fall. Big Bob Williams was dead.

With him had died the era of open and unfenced range.

Big Bob did not hear the boots moving across the floor of the big living-room. Lamplight reflected from the silver inlay on the spurs, from the glossy shine on the boots. Lamplight showed the deep grooves in the harsh face of young Matt Williams.

"For Gawd's sake, Matt, sit down!"

The boots stopped. Matt Williams smiled cynically as he studied Ag Keller. On the table beside Keller was a quart of whiskey. Keller raised the bottle and drank noisily.

"Don't hit that too hard, Ag."

"Why not?"

"Those farmers might organize and hit at us any time."

"We got guards out," Ag Keller reminded. "I'd sure cotton to know who that button was who put the lead into Tony!"

"Prob'ly some farmer."

"What was he doin' out on the range so early in the mornin'?"

"Maybe he was out rustlin' one of my steers."

"We should have fought it out with him."

"Why?"

"Well, because — Hell, he killed Tony, he did!"

"Just another hired hand with a slow gun," Matt Williams murmured. He walked to the doorway and looked at the corpse. "So the Ol' Gent with the Scythe finally knocked you down, eh, old Big Bob Williams."

Big Bob made no reply.

Matt Williams spoke again to the dead man. "I took a lot from you. You whipped me and beat me and all the time you said you were doing it for my good. You were a tough man once. But old age slowed you down, old man."

Ag Keller watched, eyes a little sick.

Matt Williams said, "All right, Big Bob, your day is done. You caused me enough hell with your beatin's an' your preachin'. Now preach a good sermon wherever you are!" Matt's voice was hard, bitter.

33

Ag Keller said, "Don't bawl him out, Matt. Hell, he cain't hear you. A man is supposed to have respect for the dead."

"Respect? Why?"

"I dunno, but a man should have."

A rider came in, said, "We buried Tony, Matt. Down in the willers along the crick."

"Good riddance."

"Wonder if he left any kin we should notify?"

"Forget that. Divide his money and belongings between you. Now get to hell out of here."

The rider left.

Ag Keller said, "Wonder where the squaw went?"

"Back to her people, I guess. Anyway, if I catch her around here, I'll give her about a fifty-yard start, and then put a .30-30 bullet into her."

Matt Williams went to the barn, got a buckskin and slung up his saddle and rode away.

Matt Williams had no eye for the beauty of this range. He had made his first move, and it was a move designed to hold intact a cattle kingdom. To the east, out on the flat country, was a burned homestead shack; in that shack, burned and black, was the body of what had once been laughing Jack Maloney. The first move had been made.

Without warning, he swung to the west, heading for a cabin situated on Hanging Woman's Creek. He rode in, his right hand high and with the palm out. Apparently the cabin was deserted. Although outwardly he was calm, inwardly there was turmoil in Matt Williams. A man could be hidden in the brush with a rifle.

Matt Williams stopped the buckskin and sat a silent saddle — a young man, big and raw-boned and holding in himself his own destiny.

Finally Williams said, "John Powers."

The brush made its sounds and a heavy-set man of about forty stepped out. He had a heavy, thick-jowled face and his lips were too thick — they were greedy lips. Now his tongue came out and ran its thick redness across the thick lips.

"You get up early," Williams said.

They were two bobcats measuring each other. Finally Powers said, "I saw a fire over toward Maloney's place. That took me into the brush. Then a while ago Sandra Smith rode by."

"A fire? Maloney's farm?"

Powers kept on watching Williams. His voice was low, "Maloney is dead. Burned to death in his cabin."

"Tough luck."

Powers asked, "What do you know about it, Williams?"

Matt Williams shrugged. "Not a thing. My men and me were home all night. The old man died last night. I'm ridin' to town to make grave preparations now. Thought I'd swing over and see you."

"About what?"

Williams looked at the farmer. "Powers, you're playing a game here, and I can't savvy just what it is. These farmers pay you for locating them on homesteads. You make money there. But it looks to me like there's something else behind this."

"You got a strong imagination."

"You locate farmers on land you know damned well won't raise crops. They pay you and then they start to starve to death. I understand that farmer over on Warm Butte left the other day."

"He did."

"Heard he sold his homestead rights to you?"

"He did."

"What do you aim to do with them?"

"That," said Jim Powers, "is my business, Williams."

Williams did not understand this well-dressed man. Powers rode a bronc like a saddleman should ride a horse, but still he did not dress like a cowpuncher — or a farmer, either. He was working his own farm but his hands were not doing the work. He had a hired man.

"Maybe," said Williams, "we could work together?"

Powers shook his head, eyes lusterless. "You're only fishing for information. You can't work with me and I can't work with you. Both of us have a little too much greed and danged too much ambition. We'd clash."

"We're clashing now."

Powers nodded. "Maloney's house didn't burn by accident."

"What can you prove?"

Powers spread his well-kept hands. "Nothing, Matt Williams. Absolutely nothing. Now I own Maloney's farm. He had a stipulation in his homestead entry that, in case of death, his farm reverts to me."

"You copper your bets. You lack in one department, though."

"And that?"

"Guns, farmer, guns!"

Powers showed a thin smile. "I have guns," he assured. "I have two fast gunmen on my side."

"Who are they?"

"That," said Powers, "is my business. You've had your say. Now ride on about your

37

business, Matt Williams."

Williams sighed, and the sigh was one of suppressed anger. And Williams said, "Big Bob is dead. So now I own the Cross in a Circle. No farmer squats on our graze. I'll look at you through the smoke of a gun. Remember that. If your game is worth-while I'll let you play in with me."

"I play a lone hand."

"Just remember Big Bob isn't alive now to hold me back."

"I judged he was dead. There was fire in the sky last night."

Williams turned the buckskin and rode away. He was big in his saddle, his back was toward John Powers. Powers was ruthless and Powers had his game, and Williams knew that a bullet can kill a man from behind as readily as it can from his front. Still, he put his back toward the dude farmer, and Powers noticed this, and inside him arose a grudging admiration.

Williams rose over the hill and the hill rose and cut him from Powers' view. He had made a bid against John Powers, and each had tested the other, and who had come out second best?

He had the unhappy feeling that John Powers had out-bested him, for he had gone to see Powers with a compromise, and Powers had not come to him. This thought was not good. He was the son of the cattle baron, and he was wealthy. He had gone to compromise with a dirt farmer, and the farmer had rebuffed him.

Anger was with him when he rode into Ringbone town. Behind the Broken Boot Café was a one room house, set apart by a small picket fence, and he opened and closed the gate and went up the gravel walk. He knocked on the door three times.

"Mildred?"

"What do you want, Matt?"

"What do I want?" Savagery was in his voice. "I want to talk to you, of course. The Old Man is dead."

"Oh, heavens."

The door opened and he entered. She wore a dressing robe and she was about twenty-two — she was blonde and slim and lovely. She had just got out of bed and the room held the sweet secret aroma of a woman. His blood quickened.

"Your dad — he's dead?"

He put his arm around her and held her close. "I didn't come to talk about the old fool." He put his hand on her chin and lifted her lips. She evaded his mouth.

"Matt, please go. People will talk."

"Let the damned fools talk. I want you. And

I'll have you, Mildred!"

Her blue eyes held tears. "You want me, Matt, but you don't love me. You have a wife, and her name is Ambition. Now please, Matt, let me go, and please leave my house."

His lips came down, crushed hers.

For a moment, then, she fought against him, her full body wiry and strong under the thin dressing robe. Then she went slack and her body pressed against his, and her lips, despite her efforts, met and blended with his.

After a while she said, "I love you, Matt."

He said nothing.

She said, "And I hate you, Matt."

FIVE

Buck McKee ate breakfast at the Broken Boot Café. He was cleaning his plate when a young man entered. He was well-dressed and his wide shoulders showed his arrogance. He took a stool.

"Coffee, Wong."

"Name no Wong. Name is Charlie."

"Trot out some coffee, Wong."

The Chinaman poured coffee. The young buckaroo cradled the warm cup between his big hands and studied Buck with a calm scrutiny. Buck got the impression that this man was eyeing him for a definite reason. The man's gaze, probing and brazen, angered the cowpuncher a little.

"Figure you'll know me the next time you see me?" Buck asked.

"I'm Matt Williams."

So this was Matt Williams, son of the old curly wolf himself, eh?

"The name," said Buck McKee, "means

41

nothing to me."

"I own the Cross in a Circle."

"Still means nothing." Buck dug in his levis for change. "How much are the damages, Charlie?"

"Thirty-five cent, cowboy."

Buck paid, said, "Good chuck." The back door opened and he could see over the swinging door that led to the kitchen. She was a beauty just as Sandra was a beauty. But where Sandra was full-bodied and dark, this girl was light-haired and thinner.

"Hello, Miss Mildred," the cook said.

"How are you this morning, Charlie?"

The girl saw Matt Williams and said, "What do you want for breakfast, Matt?" She did not await an answer. She spoke to Charlie. "Big Bob Williams died last night, Charlie."

"Big Bob — he die?"

"That's right, Chink." Matt Williams spoke abruptly. "The old man kicked the bucket. I own the Cross in a Circle now."

Charlie regarded Matt Williams with thoughtful Oriental eyes, but he said nothing. Buck was loathe to depart for he had learned much from this conversation. He turned to go and Matt Williams said, rather harshly, "Mister, what's your business in this town?"

"You speakin' to me, fella?"

"I am."

42

Buck McKee decided he did not like this arrogant young rooster.

"My business," said Buck McKee, "is my concern and nobody else's."

"You a farmer?"

"I'm not."

"There's only one cow outfit that uses this town as a base, cowboy. That's my Cross in a Circle spread. The other big outfit close is about sixty miles north, on the Little Big Horn. I could hire you if you handle a fast gun. Can you do that?"

"I've never had anybody time me," Buck said, and coldly walked out.

He felt a little angry. Trouble had heaped up on him with a suddenness. He had ridden into a range he had thought a peaceful range. Out of the night riders had come and guns had talked. He had seen fire and death, and he had held Sandra Smith in his arms. Tortilla Joe had killed a man — a Cross in a Circle gunman — and big Matt Williams had brushed his fur in the wrong direction. John Powers' letter had pulled him into trouble, and, in the letter, Powers had just invited him down for a spell, an old friend writing to another.

Well, soon he'd meet Tortilla Joe, and the Mexican would tell him much for, according to Sandra Smith, Tortilla Joe had been some

43

days loafing around Ringbone.

Where was Tortilla now?

The hour was early. Saloons and store were not yet open. An old man was sweeping the board walk in front of a saloon, and Buck got him into conversation, telling him that Big Bob Williams had died in the night.

"Kinda figgered he'd kick the bucket soon. Wonder what was wrong with him? Somethin' inside of him jes' seemed to eat him up."

"You knew him purty well?"

The old man spat. "As well as any man knew him, I reckon, an' that weren't very well. Big Bob always was stand-offish an' he never made friends with no man, just made acquaintances. Wonder what'll become of his squaw."

"Who is she?"

"Crow squaw named Many Feathers. Ol' Bob loved Many Feathers more'n any of his white women, 'peared to me. Matt has prob'ly run her off. He hates her."

"Who's that purty blonde girl down at the Broken Boot beanery?"

"She's Mildred James. Raised an' born here. Her father died about two years ago, an' she runs the café herself. They say Matt Williams would like to hook up with her. Mister, you ask a lot of questions for a stranger. You all

44

lookin' for somebody aroun' here?"

"Yes, a Mex."

"The one thet kilt Sig Rudder?"

"The same."

"You 'pear to be a right nice young feller," the swamper said. "I'd sure kinda hate to see thet Mex kill you."

"He won't kill me. Where can I find him?"

A scraggly hand made a gesture toward the southern hills. "He's somewhere out thataway. Got a camp out there, I reckon."

The hills started about a mile from Ringbone town, then rose a few thousand feet before settling down and becoming benchland. They were dotted with pine and spruce and thick buckrush.

Buck went to his bronc tied to the hitchrail in front of the Broken Boot Café. His horse needed grass and oats and a rest. Buck was unwrapping the rawhide bridle reins from around the teeth-gnawed pinepole rack when big Matt Williams came out of the café.

"Leaving town, eh?"

"Pullin' out."

Williams nodded. "You show good judgement. I can't use you — we'd never get along. You're bullheaded and so am I."

Buck nodded. "Said correct, friend. I never did cotton to taking orders, even from a woman."

"We're alike in thet respect, stranger."

Mildred James watched through the window. Buck's eyes met hers and she looked at Matt Williams.

Buck headed for the south hills. He made a mental summation of the facts he had learned since coming to Ringbone. He had met Matt Williams. The toughness of the man was easily apparent. Mixed with this toughness was a shrewdness that told of an active and strong mind.

Pumpkin-rollers had moved in on Williams' range. Range he claimed through squatter's rights, range to which he had no deeds. Farmers had come in with barbwire and plows and discs. Buck did not like farmers. He was a saddleman, first and last and always. Any man who could walk for miles and miles a day behind a walking-plow was, to put it mildly, a little crazy. Plows tore up the roots of buffalo grass. Then the wind came along and blew the topsoil away because there were no roots to hold it.

But where did John Powers fit into this? Sandra Smith had said John Powers had a homestead on a creek called Hanging Woman's Creek. Powers, being a homesteader, would be opposed to Matt Williams, and that meant trouble. Buck decided that Tortilla Joe would be loaded down with information about this deal.

Tortilla Joe had been summoned onto Ringbone range by John Powers too. Then why was not the Mexican at the Powers' farm? Why did he bed-down out here in the hills? Or was Tortilla Joe at the Powers' farm?

Tortilla Joe, if he were in these hills, would be awake by this time. Buck climbed a ridge, searching for a telltale whisp of smoke that would reveal the location of the Mexican's camping grounds. But the blue morning sky showed no smoke.

Finally he turned his tired pony. He headed for the general direction of John Powers' farm. He was riding along a coulee trail when a voice spoke from the brush.

"My ol' *amigo*, Buck McKees, no?"

Buck laughed. "Tortilla Joe, come out of the brush an' let me look at you, you old warthog!"

SIX

They rode toward John Powers' farm.

Tortilla Joe said, "For about seex months I no see you, pardner. When we spleet up in Salt Lake the Ceety, I go over aroun' Rawlins, down south."

"How did Powers know where you were?"

"Me, I dunno that." Tortilla Joe shrugged heavy shoulders. "But I get the letters from heem, an' he ask about you, an' I tell heem you up north in Montana, an' so he write to you, too?"

Buck spat and said, "I don't savvy it, pard. You played it wise. You looked the ground over before you made a play."

"I feeger you be along soon, Buck. I no want to get into trouble without you to help me."

Buck smiled. "Nice and considerate of you, Tortilla. But it 'pears to me you got in trouble with a gent named Rudder, even before I came."

Buck told about meeting the night-riders, how they had exchanged shots, and he told about meeting Miss Sandra Smith.

"Very eempolite," Tortilla Joe said. He took a small bundle out of his saddlebag. "Me, I have not had the breakfast yet."

Buck watched him unroll a tortilla and sink his white teeth into it. He then learned about Margarita at the Spoon and Fork Café.

"Maybe I marries her," Tortilla Joe said, and sighed.

"You're always going to marry some woman. Then, in about a week, you get tired of her and want to pull out, but she doesn't get tired of you — and we're both in a heck of a fix."

"I no get tired of Margarita."

Buck said, "Let's talk sense. Let's talk about this Powers fellow. Heck, I haven't seen him for ten years or so, not once you an' me an' him punched cows on the Milk River up in Montana."

"He cowboy then."

"He was a good one, too."

Tortilla Joe chewed his tortilla. "He no cowboy now."

"No, he's a farmer, they tell me."

"No farmer, either." Buck glanced at his partner.

Tortilla Joe said, "He dress beeg all the

time. New suits, an' he no wear boots — he wear shoes, all polished."

"He must look like heck follerin' a plow in that regalia."

"He no follow the plow. He hire a mans to do that. He no do nothin', I tells you, Buck."

Buck pulled in his bronc. "Wait a minute. You're shootin' too fast at me."

Tortilla Joe emphasized his words with gestures that became rather violent. "Powers, he ees workeeng some scheme, Buck. He needs two gunmens, so he sends for us. He has changed a lot. He used to be a cowboy; now he ees the beezness man, always dressed nice. He ees now a sleecker."

"I never did trust him too much," Buck had to admit. "He wrote and told me you and a bunch of his old friends would hold a reunion here. I figured I'd look you up an' we'd head over across the mountains into Utah an' ride winterherd for ol' Marty Enright an' his Broken Leg outerfit an' winter there."

"He write same to me, too."

"Any of the other boys show up?"

"None of them. An' I tells you why, Buck. He no write to them. He want us, because of our guns."

"Shag us into somethin', eh? Well, let's see what he's got to say for himself."

The rest of the ride was made in silence. Buck and Tortilla were glad to be back together again. Both rode poor, trail-tired horses. If they pulled out for Utah they would need fresh broncs.

They had left the benchland and were now on the flat country that bordered each bank of Ringbone Creek. The little cowtown was slightly west of them, back toward the hills that, in turn, arose and became the Big Horn Mountains. The farmers were, with a few exceptions, located on the north bank of Ringbone Creek. Hanging Woman's Creek, where John Powers had his homestead, angled in from the northwest, and entered Ringbone Creek a mile or so below the town of Ringbone.

"Yonder, Buck, ees the Cross in a Circle *rancho*."

Tortilla Joe pointed toward the west. Buck looked and said, "I can't see no buildings."

"They are behind the hills from you."

Buck said, "I don't give a damn where the outfit is. If John Powers has lied to us, I'm workin' the son over with my fists."

"I weel beat you to heem."

"My meat," Buck said. "If he's jobbed us, God help him!"

"He tough mans."

"I can take him. First, we'll give him a chance to talk, though."

"That house she ees hees."

Powers had built a nice house in the cottonwood trees. Most of the farmers built of native log because they were too poor to buy lumber. But John Powers had built a rambling house of lumber and it was painted a neat light green. It was quite a spread.

"He must have some dinero," Buck grunted.

"He buys up the farmers' lands when they pull out. Soon thing you know he weel own the valley."

A collie barked as they rode into the yard and John Powers came out of the house. He was immaculately dressed and he shook hands with each. Then he invited them into the house. Buck entered a big living room that had new rugs and a new carpet, and the furniture, also, was new.

"You married now, John?" Buck joked.

"Have one of the farmers' daughters come in and clean. Her name is Sandra Smith, and she lives a few miles from here."

Buck nodded, face deadpan. For some reason he didn't like the idea that Sandra was a charwoman for this man. Tortilla Joe had made an understatement when he claimed that Powers had changed. He was a cowpuncher no longer; now he was a businessman, brusque and active.

"Have some coffee, men?"

"If you can spike mine," Buck said.

They sat around the table watching each other. Buck stirred his coffee with his forefinger but John Powers stirred his with a silver spoon.

"Where are the rest of the boys?" Buck asked suddenly.

"They'll be along soon, I guess."

"I been here for four days or so," Tortilla Joe said. Powers sent a displeased glance toward the Mexican. "So I heard," he murmured. "Why didn't you look me up when you came on this range? I had good chuck and a good bed for you."

"Me, I waits for Buck."

"Heard you killed Sig Rudder?"

Tortilla Joe shook his head dolefully. "He make me keel heem."

"Good riddance," John Powers said. "Hope you kill more of those Williams' scissor-bills."

That sentence, hotly spoken, clarified all doubts that might have been in Buck's mind, and he knew now, for certain, that he and Tortilla Joe had been tricked into coming into Ringbone. Powers wanted gundogs. This thought brought anger to him but he kept it from his voice.

"Powers," he said, "what's your game?"

"I don't follow you, Buck."

53

Buck stood up. He leaned forward and pounded the table. "Don't put on a dumb act for me, Powers. You ain't gonna have no ol'time cowboy reunion. You want two gunmen, an' you figured that if me an' Tortilla Joe showed up, you'd have those gunmen. Well, here we are."

Powers got to his feet. He walked the length of the room, turned, looked at them; his smile was paper-thin.

"Yes, McKee, I need gunmen. I tricked you two into coming on Ringbone range." John Powers raised his hand to cut off Buck's words. "Don't get hot under the collar until we talk further. How would you like to make fifty bucks a week? That adds up to two hundred a month. And found."

Tortilla Joe had to grunt.

Buck's eyes narrowed. The most he had ever drawn in wages was fifty per month. Most of the time he and Tortilla Joe worked for twenty or thirty bucks a month. Now this man — this former cowpuncher — was offering him fifty bucks a week!

Buck spoke to John Powers. "A gunman, eh?"

"Gunhand wages."

Buck said, "Against the Cross in a Circle spread?"

"Right."

"This land ain't worth that much," Buck said. "There's lots of farming land that's much better for the plow. Where did you get all this dinero and what's behind your wantin' this land? There's more behind it than making a farm out of it all."

"You read something into it that's not there. I want these farms and I'll get them. I'm fighting two forces here. I'm fighting to get these farmers out so they will sell deeds to me. I'm fighting the Williams' spread, too. Only the farmers don't know I'm fighting them on the quiet. They think I'm their friend."

Buck remembered Sandra Smith's hot words about John Powers. One farmer surely did not trust Powers.

"How about it, McKee?"

"Not for me," Buck said.

Powers turned sharp eyes on Tortilla Joe. "And you, Tortilla?"

"Buck rides out. Me, I rides weeth heem."

"Three hundred per month."

"No."

"No."

"Three fifty?"

Buck said, "Not for me."

"Nor me, either."

Powers spread his hands. "I'll make it four hundred. I'll go no higher. That's a lot of dough."

Buck said, "Well, now —" and he moved closer. Powers smiled, thinking the lanky cowpuncher had reconsidered. He moved close to shake hands. But Buck said, "Mister, put up your fists, 'cause I aim to beat the hell outa you for trickin' us!"

Powers snarled, his fist lashed out.

SEVEN

When the squaw left the Cross in a Circle, she headed for Pete Smith's farm. She liked Sandra Smith and she wanted to talk to somebody; Sandra had talked to her once or twice in Ringbone town. The rest of the white women would not speak to her, even though she was Big Bob's squaw.

Matt Williams' boot had given her a bloody nose and the right side of her face was swollen. He had kicked her hard. She hated Matt Williams with the same degree of emotion that she had loved his father. She carried a sack of grub, and she had a Winchester .30-30 rifle. Her thinking was rather limited and the sudden turn of events had disturbed her mental equilibrium.

She had wanted to give Big Bob a good funeral, but now that was impossible. Her people would not accept her wholeheartedly — she had left her tribe to travel with the pale faces; she had been a white man's squaw.

She did not know just what to do next. First, she would talk with Sandra Smith.

Within her aching breast was a demand that she get even with Matt Williams. Her jaw would be swollen and sore for weeks and she would have a black eye. But the pain in her face fell far short of the intensity of her inner turmoil. Big Bob, her bulwark, was gone; he was cold clay, and the earth would soon claim him. . . . She could go no further. She stopped, put down her rifle and pack-bag, and she sat beside a rock on a hillside, and she wept as only broken-hearted women can weep.

Finally she slept, and when she wakened, it was dawn. She had been dead-tired. Night after night she had nursed Big Bob Williams, and utter fatigue — a deadly tiredness — had been in her. Only Time and rest and forgetfulness would erase that fatigue.

She stood up, and looked at the basin below.

There was a fire down below her. She knew, immediately, that Matt Williams and his riders had burned a nester's outfit, and she knew that the outfit had belonged to a man named Jack Maloney. She had seen Maloney once in Ringbone town. She had liked his clean-cut, almost boyish face; the confident manner he had assumed. She knew that Maloney was dead.

Matt would turn his valley into a valley of raw red hell.

There was still the dogged determination to see Sandra Smith. So she went again toward the Smith farm. Pete Smith came out of the house with a rifle. He was a thin, unshaven man — a homely man with a crooked nose. He said, "You're Big Bob Williams' woman, ain't you?"

"Big Bob, he dead."

Pete Smith turned and looked toward Maloney's farm. "Now I savvy the fire," he murmured. "So now Matt Williams owns the Cross in a Circle."

"Where your daughter?"

"She rode towards the fire."

The squaw shook her heavy head with dour slowness. "She should not do that. Matt he find her. Matt he mean man. He kick me in the face and do this to me." She touched her black-and-blue cheek.

"He'd best not lay a hand on my girl."

"I wait for her. I wanna see her."

"Come inside."

"No, I wait here."

The squaw sank to the soil and sat cross-legged in the dust of the yard. Pete Smith walked up the slope, carrying his rifle. When Sandra rode in she saw Many Feathers and she dismounted and ran to her.

"Many Feathers, what are you doing here? And what happened to your face?"

She told the dark-haired girl what had happened.

Pete Smith said, "You can't stay here, squaw."

"Why not?" Sandra challenged.

"We got enough trouble as it is. Matt hates this squaw. If he finds out she's at our shack he'll hit at us to get at her!"

"We'll defend her!"

Pete Smith turned his faded blue eyes on Many Feathers. The squaw was reaching a mental decision. Many Feathers stood up.

"I go," she said. "I see your side, Mister Smith. I no want to get friends into trouble." She looked at Sandra. "Where is the Mexican?"

Sandra was puzzled. "What Mexican?"

"The one he kill Sig Rudder, the dirty thief!"

"Oh, the one they call Tortilla Joe. He was around town yesterday. Margarita would know. She's sweet on him."

Many Feathers said, "Tortilla Joe, he enemy of Matt Williams. He kill Rudder, and Rudder he top gunman for Matt. Matt never let that Mexican ride out of Ringbone valley alive."

"You think he won't?" Sandra asked.

"I know he no let him. If he let him get away free then the rule of Matt will be busted."

Pete Smith bit off a chew of Horseshoe. "By golly, daughter, I believe she is right, at that. It makes logic. Matt is awful proud. He made the boast that Sig Rudder was the fastest man he had with a gun. Tortilla Joe knocked Rudder into Kingdom Come with a bullet. Tortilla Joe is marked in Matt Williams' book."

"That right," Many Feathers said.

Sandra asked, "You intend to join forces with Tortilla Joe?"

"I do that."

"Do you need some supplies?"

"I got shells for rifle an' I got grub in sack."

"I don't like this one bit," Sandra stated positively. "Dad, she can stay here."

But Many Feathers shook her head. "Your father he right first time. I fight from brush. Mexican no want me, I fight alone."

There was hate in her voice — steely, grating hate. This made Pete Smith grim and uncertain, for he had never heard any woman, white or Indian, speak with such hate.

Many Feathers walked away.

Sandra caught her. "You can't go on foot, Many Feathers. You can have my horse. I can't let you go away on foot."

"I take horse, but I bring him back some time. I no take saddle; just the horse."

When Many Feathers made up her mind, apparently she would not change it. She would not take a saddle. Sandra helped her mount the rawboned old horse and then handed the squaw the rifle and her sack of grub. Many Feathers guided the bronc with a rope tied around his lower jaw. She made a ludicrous figure on the horse.

"I bring horse back soon."

"You be careful, and you watch yourself."

Pete Smith came out of the house and stood beside his daughter.

"What happened at the fire? We was so busy arguin' with that redskin I never got to ask you about Maloney. I figger Maloney's dead."

"He burned in the fire."

"Matt Williams is a wild man now that his dad is dead."

She told about meeting Buck McKee. Peter Smith chewed and spat and watched Many Feathers ride off into the early morning.

Many Feathers rode into Ringbone town.

Margarita was cooking at the Spoon and Fork. No, she did not know where Tortilla Joe was. He didn't have sense enough to even come to town for a good supper of frijoles and enchiladas, complete with mescal. She hated all men right now.

"Why do you want to see my man, Indian?"

"I want to tell him something about Matt," the squaw lied. Margarita had too much jealousy in her voice.

"You tell me. I'll tell him. I don't want no woman foolin' aroun' with my man, savvy?"

"You loco. I no see him."

"You'd better not try to shine up to him."

With difficulty Many Feathers remounted. She did not ride toward the south, for she figured Margarita would be watching her; she left town toward the north, apparently heading back for the Cross in a Circle. Once out of Margarita's sight, she swung around Ringbone to the west, and headed for the southern hills.

She missed Tortilla Joe. She rode too far to the west. Tortilla Joe saw her through his field glasses but he, of course, did not know she was looking for him.

Then he dismissed the redskin from his mind, for his field glasses had picked up Buck McKee heading toward the hills.

And he rode down to meet his own partner.

EIGHT

Tortilla Joe had seen Buck McKee in a number of fights before, both gun fights and fists fights. But never had he seen his partner deal out such punishment as Buck handed to John Powers.

When Powers hit, he intended to smash home the first blow by trickery, but his trickery did not work. Buck McKee ducked and the man's fist went over his head. Powers walked into Buck's left hook, curving in and hitting Powers in the belly.

"You gets heem, Buck!" Tortilla Joe yelled.

Buck dimly heard his partner's cheering words. Powers was dressed like a soft city man, but he was no dude. Any man who could take a left hook like the one that Buck handed out, and then come back the way Powers came back — that man was not soft. Buck knew then he had a fight on his hands.

Anger was a savage fire in Buck, burning with a brittle flame. He controlled this anger, though — coldness would win this fight, and blinding anger would lose it. John Powers had tricked him and Tortilla Joe. Powers had put them both into danger without taking the courtesy to advise them, ahead of time, that danger awaited them. His trickery was dirty, underhanded, and unforgivable because they'd once been friends.

They knocked down the table, and dishes and pots went sliding down with a loud clatter. Buck got his boot in a cooking pot, and his boot stuck. He kicked to get the pot off his boot. Powers nailed him with a hard hook.

Buck went down.

Tortilla Joe said, "I gets heem!" and started forward. "This is my fight!" Buck gritted.

"All right, you takes heem, then," Tortilla Joe conceded.

And Buck took him.

John Powers wasn't a pretty sight. Buck had broken his nose, his left ear was ripped partly loose, and one eye would soon be swollen shut. He lay on his side and he spat blood. He panted like a wind-broken old workhorse.

"McKee, I'll kill you for this!"

"I'm a hard gent to kill," Buck reminded. To Tortilla Joe he said, "Pick up all the weapons you can find. This gent might try to shoot us from behind as we ride out."

"I get hees revolver an' hees rifles, Buck."

Buck went outside and washed in the horse-trough. His head reeled. The cold water helped restore his equilibrium. He had given John Powers what he had asked for. His knuckles would be stiff for some days, but not as sore as John Powers' face.

Tortilla Joe came out, carrying a rifle and a pistol.

"Rider comin'," Buck grunted.

The rider was a short, heavy-set man with an ugly face. He rode a blue roan that toted the Cross in a Circle brand. Dull eyes settled on Tortilla and Joe.

"The old Mex gunslinger hisself, eh?" He purred the words nastily.

Buck asked, "Who are you, fella?"

The dull eyes switched back to Buck Mc-Kee. "Not that it's a danged bit of your biz-ness, fella, what my handle is, but I'll tell you you are talkin' to Ag Keller, who works for the Williams' iron."

Tortilla Joe said, "You a pal of Sig Rudder, no? I see you an' Rudder een town together oncet."

"Right you are, spic."

Keller's voice was purringly insulting. The word spic registered and made blood flush the Mexican's big jowls.

Buck murmured, "Ride a tight saddle,

66

chum." His eyes lifted to meet those of Ag Keller. "I'm Buck McKee. This Mexican and me are partners. A man hit at him, he has me to tangle with, too."

"Real chummy, eh?"

Buck said, "What are you doin' here, Keller?"

Keller said, "Done heard a lot of noise in the cabin, so rode down to investigate. From the looks of your mug, McKee, I'd say that John Powers got the best of you."

"You ain't seen Powers yet," Buck corrected.

They started for their broncs. But Ag Keller's words stopped them for a moment longer.

"When did you ride into this range, McKee?"

"Last night."

"From which direction?"

Buck said, "That's my bizness."

Keller said, quietly, "It might be my bizness, and the bizness of Matt Williams, savvy?"

"How so?"

Keller jabbed a thumb toward Tortilla Joe. "This Mex pard of your'n shot down a Cross in a Circle man. Williams ain't forgettin' that. Big Bob Williams is dead, and Matt rods the iron now. Orders are for the Mex to be killed.

He's run against Matt, and he ain't leavin' Ringbone Valley alive."

Tortilla Joe had a grimy hand on his holstered gun. "Maybe, Meester Keller, you want to try your hand, no?"

Keller showed a ghost of a smile. "Not against the two of you, spic. Maybe later. . . ." He looked at Buck McKee. "There's trouble here, McKee. Last night one of the nester's shacks accidentally caught fire. Nester burned in it. Last night, too, one of the Cross in a Circle riders got killed."

Buck played dumb. "Killed? Horse fall on him or somethin'?"

Keller shook his heavy head. "This fella was shot out of saddle in the night."

Buck remembered the riders sweeping down on him. He remembered the flat wicked stab of his .45 and he remembered the rider sagging against the saddle's fork as they thundered on. Buck McKee kept his face deadpan.

"I don't foller you," he said.

"You ride in from the north, eh?"

"South," Buck said.

In Ag Keller's eyes Buck read a slow cynicism.

"This rider came from the north," Keller murmured. "He shot an' killed a man named Tony."

"I dunno him, Keller."

Keller turned his bronc, said, "Matt Williams is blockin' the trails out of Ringbone. This valley is ringed in with Cross in a Circle steel."

Buck said, "A man could gun his way through."

"He might. Then again he might not."

Keller lifted his blue roan and loped away. Buck went to saddle and Tortilla Joe mounted. They loped down Ringbone Creek, and came to a grove of cottonwood trees that spread a cool blanket of shade. Cross in a Circle cattle had bedded down in these trees, good blooded cows with strong calves. The Hereford strain had been mixed with that of the Longhorn and the result was a cow with stamina for the hard Wyoming winters and with good foraging ability.

Buck said, "We rest our broncs."

"Keller, he feegure you keel Tony," Tortilla Joe said.

"I killed him. He shot at me and I shot back."

"Matt Weeliams, he no like you either, now. He no like me from the time I shoots the Seeg Rudder."

Buck said, "Brother, we're in trouble. We thought we were going on a picnic — an old timers' reunion. Instead it's a gunsmoke party.

We could drift out."

Tortilla Joe shook his head. "They would turn us back or keel us. Both of us have crossed the Matt Williams."

"That's right."

Buck gave this some thought. Powers was against him, and Williams was against him. And Ringbone Valley was ringed with guns against him and his partner.

He had killed Tony, but that had been in self-defense. Yes, and Tortilla Joe had got rid of Rudder; also, in self-defense.

He had had one bright moment while on this range. That had been when he had met lovely Sandra Smith. Their meeting, though, had been anything but conventional.

"Sandra Smith hates Powers," he said.

"Why?"

"I don't know. I'm ridin' over to talk to her."

On the way to the Smith farm they saw a rider along the base of the hills, about two miles away. Tortilla Joe fixed his field glasses on the rider and said it was a woman. A big woman he said; looked like a squaw. Riding bareback. The rider went into the hills and out of sight.

Buck said, "That must be Smith's spread. We're about a mile from Maloney's shack. Sandra said she lived a mile away."

"You know a lots about her," Tortilla Joe joked.

Buck gave his partner a sudden stabbing glance. He liked women a lot, but he didn't want one — not at this stage of the game. There were still hills to ride over and new range to see.

"I know as much as I'm goin' to know."

NINE

Sandra Smith was feeding her chickens when they rode into the yard. The clean beauty of the girl registered on Buck McKee, even though he deliberately steeled himself against her appeal.

"Mr. McKee — What happened to your face?"

Buck tried to grin. "John Powers done whipped me," he joked.

"Oh!"

The grain bucket fell to the ground. Golden wheat spilled out into the dust. The chickens fell to with great ambition.

"He whipped you, you say?"

Pete Smith had come out of the house. "Always figgered mebbe Powers was a tough gent with his fists," the farmer said slowly. "From the looks of your face, fella, I guessed right for oncet."

Tortilla Joe said, "He didn't tell you all, folks. He laid John Powers out cold an' he

72

wrecked hees shack. Eef you theenk Buck looks bad you should see John Powers."

"Hope you kilt him," Pete Smith grumbled.

Sandra spoke to her father. "This is Mr. McKee, Dad. And this is Mr. Tortilla Joe, who killed — er, shot down Sig Rudder."

Pete Smith shook hands with Buck. Buck and his partner dismounted and were invited into the house. Buck told about the deal John Powers had pulled on him and his partner. Pete Smith listened and nodded. Powers, he said for the tenth time, was a skunk — a human skunk.

"He's got some scheme up his sleeve and it ain't for the good of us farmers, you can bet your last dollar on that."

Tortilla Joe asked, "What ees hees scheme, gentlemans?"

"I sure don't know," Pete Smith replied. "He got us farmers in here and now he's bought up the homestead rights of them that has pulled stakes an' left Ringbone."

"He wants the land for some reason," Buck said. "He's got a scheme to get hold of it and he's usin' you farmers."

Sandra asked, "Wonder if he's joined forces with Matt Williams?"

They considered that premise for a short time. Buck told about meeting Ag Keller and the warning Keller had given them. Suddenly Sandra gasped.

"Oh, Mr. Tortilla, I almost forgot. There was somebody here looking for you not more than an hour ago."

"Who was he?"

"It was a she, not a he. She was Big Bob Williams' squaw, Many Feathers."

"I see big womans ride away on horse when we rides in here. I no even know thees squaw. Yet she look for me, eh?"

Buck smiled. "You got too many women, pard. You've only been here a few days and already you got two women — Margarita and this Crow squaw."

"Thees ees no joke, Buck."

Sandra told about giving the squaw a horse and how her face had been swollen. "Matt Williams kicked her, I guess. He ran her off the Cross in a Circle the minute his father died."

Pete Smith suddenly asked, "You boys runnin' out of Ringbone Valley?"

Buck McKee said, "Look at it from our angle, Mr. Smith. We were tricked in here by John Powers. He wanted us to gun with him, but we don't sell our guns. My partner here has killed a man — a Cross and Circle man. He didn't want to kill that man."

"That ees right, mens."

74

Buck said, "We have nothing at stake here to fight over. You own a farm, the other farmers have property — they have a reason for fighting. But we own nothing but our horses and saddles and our shirts and pants."

Sandra flared, "And you want to own nothing, I take it!"

The ferocity of her tone caused the partners to stare at her. It was some moments before Buck McKee could find his tongue.

"That's right, Miss Sandra. The more you own the worse you feel. When you don't own nothin', you ain't got no worries."

"Hogwash!" Sandra said unexpectedly.

Pete Smith smiled. "Women always want a man to take on some burdens, men. They ain't happy unless they got a man working."

"Dad, that isn't true. But what fun is life unless one has responsibilities? The only true happiness one gets is in making somebody else happy."

Buck said, "I suppose I should get shot and killed just to make some farmer I don't know happy?"

She stood up and put her hands on the table. "Buck McKee, that isn't what I meant, and you know it! Buck, use your brains! Matt Williams isn't going to let you two ride out of Ringbone alive! You've gone against him and Matt is a proud man. If you two get the best of him he'd be the laughing stock of Ringbone Valley, and he's got to make an example of you two! Otherwise, his power is broken, and two drifting cowpunchers broke it!"

"We can get out," Tortilla Joe said.

"How?" challenged Sandra.

Buck said, "There's always a dark night. A man can ride through any of a hundred coulees and get out of Ringbone."

"You'd — run?"

Buck smiled thinly. "It might be runnin' to you, Miss Sandra. You don't have to draw and shoot a gun, and you won't be the one who has to pull that gun a shade ahead of the other fellow — or be dead. It ain't runnin' to me. It's just common sense."

Now Pete Smith spoke. "You two won't get out alive. Williams has got gunmen on his payroll. They're killers, jest like Ag Keller's a killer. They know all the trails."

"That," said Buck, "remains to be seen."

They left the Smith homestead. Sandra smiled at Buck as she said goodbye, but her smile, he knew, was only a mask to hide her real feelings. While he liked her, she had a stubborn streak, he realized — it could cause the man who married her a lot of trouble. And it could cause her much trouble, too.

Pete Smith merely said, "Good luck, buckaroos."

But Buck detected a sort of sadness in the lanky farmer's words. He got the feeling that these farmers were looking desperately for a leader.

Once Buck glanced back. Pete had gone into the house but Sandra still watched. Buck lifted his hand a little. She did not wave back. Then the cottonwood trees hid her.

Tortilla Joe said, "She ees a leetle beet mad, Buck."

"All women are mad most of the time," Buck philosophized.

"Sandra, she like you."

Buck said nothing. He remembered her brown eyes and he saw the fullness of her, the rise of her breasts, the way she filled her shirt and her levis. But above these personal qualities there was the measure of scorn in her eyes. She was proud and she was good and she was strong — yet she was as soft as the prairie wind caressing the sagebrush.

TEN

They buried Big Bob Williams that afternoon in Ringbone town.

The cowman's body was lowered into the grave in a simple wooden casket made by the local carpenter.

Matt Williams stood beside the grave with a stern, emotionless face.

An era had ended.

The era of King Cow — when cow was king — was gone. The longhorn had replaced the buffalo and the cowpuncher had replaced the redskins. King Cow had had his day. He had come into power after the Civil War. Now he was following the buffalo off open range. Within twenty years open range would be completely gone. Gone before the plows and the fences of the farmers. That was only proper; a part of history. The buffalo had had his heyday. King Cow and the cowmen had had theirs, too.

Although Big Bob had been known the

length and breadth of the Territory not many people came to see him given to the earth. For one thing his friends had not had time to come from any distance. Some of them, in fact, had not even heard that Big Bob had died.

Matt Williams wanted his father's body out of the way. Matt Williams had a chore to accomplish here in Ringbone Valley.

The casket sank into the ground and the grave-digger started to throw sod on it. Matt got his bronc and rode the half-mile from the cemetery into Ringbone town. His men rode behind him, saying very little.

None of the farmers attended the funeral.

Most of the Cross in a Circle men were out in the hills that surrounded Ringbone town. Matt Williams was making sure that two men — two drifters who had defied his rule — would not be able to sneak out of Ringbone.

His men dismounted in front of the closest saloon. Matt rode down to the office of Lawyer Hankins. There he put Big Bob's will on probate. The lawyer read the will and said, "He leaves five thousand to the squaw. Where is she?"

Matt Williams smiled. "She left the country."

The lawyer studied him through thick glasses. "It might hold up the procedure a little. The county court will make a search for her to settle the will."

"She might be dead by now," Matt said.

He should have killed the squaw. Why hadn't he killed her? He thought, I must be getting soft in the head. I should have killed her.

"You run the outfit as you see fit," the lawyer told him. "From all angles it is your cow-outfit, Matt."

Matt Williams stood up, said, "I figured that, lawyer."

Outside, he breathed deeply of the clean good air, and this made him remember Big Bob, down there in the ground with a ton of dirt on him. For a moment, then, something akin to pity flashed through Big Bob's son; this feeling, though, was short of life. Big Bob had softened a lot toward the last when the Grim Reaper had come closer. He had not wanted to fight the farmers. Well, the farmers would have a fight now.

John Powers came out of the doctor's office.

"You fall under a disc?" Matt Williams asked scornfully.

He had expected antagonism to color Powers' eyes. Instead, he saw something there that surprised him a little. It was a scheming, brooding look of speculation.

"I ran into a set of fists," Powers said.

"Who owned them?"

"A guy named Buck McKee."

Williams nodded. "I've heard of him. I thought he had come into this basin to side your damned nesters."

Powers did not answer that. "I want to talk to you some time, Williams. I got something that might interest you."

Matt Williams gave him a slow raking glance. Now why would this sodbuster want to bargain with him and what would they talk about?

"Only thing about you that could interest me, Powers, is that you drag outa this country, and take your damn' farmers with you."

Powers turned suddenly, and walked away. Matt Williams heard the jingle of tugs, the rattle of wheels, and he looked down the street. The Bighorn Stage had just rounded the corner by the General Store. The driver waved at him, then pulled his rig to a halt in front of the hotel.

"All out, passengers. The end of the line."

Two passengers came from the depths of the dirty stage. One was a girl of about twenty, painted and brazen, who lifted her skirt a little too high when she descended. The proprietor of the local saloon stepped forward and introduced himself. He and the girl then went toward his emporium.

The second passenger was a man of about fifty. He was short and pot-bellied, and he wore a blue suit, crumpled now from the long trip. He dusted himself, looked around, and then poked a new cigar between his red fat lips.

He looked at Matt Williams.

His gaze, though, was impersonal, and it went past the owner of the Cross in a Circle. With cold scrutiny the small eyes, half-hidden under fat brows, took in the cowtown.

"Here's your suitcase, fella," the driver said.

The man said, authoritatively, "Take it over to the hotel. I'll pay you there."

The stage driver put the suitcase on the ground. Then he said, "To hell with you, bucko. I'm not your slave." He climbed onto the seat and trotted away with noisy tugs, dust rising from his stage's wheels.

The newcomer smiled, but the smile was not an easy one. He started toward the hotel door, carrying his suitcase. Just outside the door he met John Powers who said, "Fine day, sir."

"Fine day, sir," the man returned.

Powers said, "Hope you have a nice stay, stranger."

"I will have." The stranger mouthed his

cigar and said, in a very low voice, "I'll see you later, Powers."

"Nice town," Powers said loudly, and went out onto the sidewalk.

To the casual observer it would seem that John Powers was welcoming a stranger to Ringbone. The stranger went into the hotel and registered as Jacob Mudd.

Powers went to the Broken Boot Café. There Mildred James waited on him. Powers tried to get her into a conversation. He was doing all right until Matt Williams came in. For some reason, Mildred James suddenly lost desire for conversation with him.

She did not talk with Matt Williams, either.

Williams ordered in a low voice. Powers finished his coffee and went outside. Cross in a Circle riders, for some reason, seemed to be converging on the Broken Boot Café.

They had all been drinking. Not drunk, not boisterous, but a little under the influence — a cold hard-grained influence that made them clip their words, that made them surly.

Mildred James frowned as they poured whiskey into coffee. Matt Williams saw that frown and he deliberately spiked his coffee.

"Matt?"

"Yes?"

"I'm selling out the café, Matt."

"Then you're leavin'?"

"Do you want me to leave?"

"Make up your own mind, gal."

The moment had passed. He had said the wrong thing. He was instantly aware of this, and it increased his coldness.

"I'm leaving," she said.

He said, "Well, then you're leaving."

They looked at each other. He judged she was close to tears. He had drunk just enough to make him want to hurt somebody. He wanted to hurt her.

"Drink up, men," he said tersely.

ELEVEN

That night Buck McKee and Tortilla Joe tried to ride out of Ringbone Valley. They ran into a stone wall of resistance — a wall of ugly guns. Because of the resistance, they both grew angry and decided to fight Matt Williams.

It happened in this manner: Matt Williams had on his payroll a half-breed Sioux named Big Moccasins. He had big feet but he had silent feet. He also had the nose of a wolfhound and the ears of a cougar. Williams had given him specific orders to kill Buck McKee and Tortilla Joe, and to keep them from skipping out of Ringbone Valley. Big Moccasins wanted a hundred dollars. He had with him three Cross in a Circle men, and he cut ahead of Buck and Tortilla with these men and they waylaid the two cowpunchers in the rough country and turned them back into the basin.

Buck did not know it until the next day,

but one of his bullets — or a bullet from Tortilla Joe's rifle — killed the half-breed called Big Moccasins. He would never have known it had not the other Cross in a Circle men taken the half-breed's body into town for burial.

Big Moccasins had been high on a ridge. He had shot down, but he had not adjusted his sights; his lead had plowed into the earth ahead of Buck's bronc. Buck had left saddle fast, with Tortilla Joe on his spurs. They had fought it out from the safety of some boulders, and they had driven off the Cross in a Circle men. The fight had lasted about an hour.

"There they ees go, Buck. We can ride out of the basin now, señor."

Buck sat on the ground, long legs running out in front of him as he put new cartridges into his rifle's magazine. A trickle of blood had dried on his swollen left cheek. A bullet had knocked a sliver out of a rock about a foot from his head.

"Yeah," he said, "we whupped them."

"Now we can ride out."

Buck seemed interested in his rifle. The moon was rising and slanting rays of golden light were beginning to illuminate this rough range of boulders and rocks. Tortilla Joe watched him and crunched a tortilla.

"What you say, Buck?"

"What do you say, pard?"

Tortilla Joe sighed. "Me, my papa he teach me not to runs from no mans, Buck. We are free to do the ride on out of here. But steel we leave behin' John Powers. Yes, an' Matt Weeliams, too. Both trick us. Both want to keel us."

Buck nodded. "Keep on talkin', amigo."

"There ees Sandra — hola, amigo, what a beauty she ees, that *muchachita!*"

"Not for me." Hurriedly.

"Not for Tortilla Joe, either. Jes' the same, she ees a woman, an' when we rides out — hola, she ees alone. And then, *también,* there ees Margarita."

"Oh, yes," Buck said. "Don't forget Margarita, by all means!"

"Margarita she ees make the good tortilla."

Buck said, "Let's stop kiddin' ourselves, Tortilla. We can get outa here but I don't cotton to goin' in this manner, for some reason. Maybe I got a little pride or somethin' but I hate like hell to be run out of Ringbone by anybody."

"Me, I ees say the same theeng, Buck"

Accordingly they had mounted and had ridden into the cowtown. They came into the town at daybreak. Margarita invited them in and made coffee. She was so big she looked

87

like a small elephant waddling around.

Margarita kept up a running conversation. She wanted to talk about Matt Williams. He claimed he would run Ringbone Valley and when he got done no farmers would be located on homesteads. He also said he'd get even with those two drifters — that Mexican and that gent named McKee.

"He say that, honey?" Tortilla Joe asked.

"So they tell me. But eet ees time I opens the restaurant. You mens come for the dinner, no?"

"We'll pay for our breakfasts," Buck said.

"No pay."

She put her hands behind her back and shook her dark head emphatically. "Both of you are my friends, señores."

A few minutes later, fed and almost normal again, the partners rode out of Ringbone, heading for the Smith farm. It was a wonderful morning. Meadowlarks sang in the high grass along the creek and calves ran and played, tails high as they galloped.

Buck breathed deeply and said, "How can man be so ornery an' mean, Tortilla Joe, when the Good Lord is so good to him? Look at this large fine morning."

"Look who ees come on the horseback," Tortilla Joe said.

All the peacefulness of the morning departed.

"Ag Keller, eh?"

"I ride toward the heels, Buck."

Tortilla Joe rode toward the foothills and, when he had gone about three hundred feet, he reined his bronc around and stopped, facing Buck McKee who sat his horse on the trail.

It was too late to back out, so Ag Keller pulled his bronc to a halt on the other side of Buck, thus getting the cowpuncher between him and Tortilla Joe. But Buck killed this move by putting his bronc ahead a little, then turning him. By this time Tortilla Joe had his Winchester lying across the fork of his old saddle.

Buck said, "Goin' some place, Keller?"

"That Mex has the drop on me," Keller growled.

Buck said, "He'll keep a sight on you, too." He seemed lazy and in this laziness was an alert deception. "Maybe you're headin' into the hills to check up on your guards out there, eh?"

"I don't foller you, McKee."

"I think you do." Buck still used that same low voice. "We ran into some of them last night. We could have rode through after the ruckus. We sat there an' chewed the fat among ourselves and decided to go farmin' instead."

"Farmin'?"

"Sure," Buck said, eyes on the gunman. "Lotsa purty girls are farmin'. We like purty girls, savvy?"

"You talk like a fool, fella!"

Buck said, over his shoulder, "Keep that Winchester on this son, Tortilla Joe." Then Buck said, "Williams tried to kill us up there."

"Williams? Matt spent the night at the ranch, fellow."

Buck said, "There was a fire down in the basin. We saw it from the rimrock. Matt had his men in the Broken Boot. They rode out in a body. Later on a nester's shack burned. Let me tell you a little secret, Ag Keller."

Keller did not know just what to think about this tall cowpuncher.

"Jes' like ol' school days, eh? A little secret?"

Buck nodded. "When you men burned down Maloney's shack the other night you rode plumb into a rider who shot down one of your men, a gent named Tony. Well, Keller, here's the secret — that rider was me."

"I kinda figgered that, McKee. Tony was a good friend of mine. I don't aim to sit here —"

"You won't *sit* that saddle long!" Buck gritted.

Buck's right hook caught the gunman on the side of the face, and knocked him out of saddle. He landed on his side, and he reached for his gun, but the .45 had slipped out of holster. Buck was on the ground; his boot went out; the .45 slid out of Ag Keller's reach.

Keller sat up and spat blood. He looked at the .45. Then he got to his feet.

"Fella, you'll die for this!"

"Put up your fists, Cross in a Circle man!"

Keller made no move to put up his fists. He spoke hoarsely. "I'm no man to use his fists. Fists settle nothin', fella. I work with a gun or not at all. Your friend has the drop on me. I have no short-gun. I won't fight with fists."

"All right," Buck said tersely. He got the .45, sun twinkled on it, but Keller did not catch it. It went past him and landed handle-down in the sod.

Keller said, "I've changed my mind. There's two of you an' only one of me. This might be a trap. I get the gun an' the Mex shoots me from behind. There'll be another time."

Tortilla Joe had ridden over and he shrugged and looked at Buck. "What can a man he do een a case like this?"

"One thing," Buck gritted. "This!"

He grabbed Keller's shoulders. He turned

the man savagely. His right boot came up and smacked Keller in the seat of his pants. Keller stumbled ahead, fell down, rolled over, and swore. Anger and shame made his face livid.

"You still don't wanta fight?" Buck demanded.

Keller got to his feet and went to his horse and climbed into saddle. Tortilla Joe had already taken the gunman's Winchester out of its saddle boot.

Keller gave them each a black look, dug in his spurs, and loped toward Ringbone town. Tortilla Joe looked at Buck McKee. His eyes were thoughtful.

"He no coward, Buck."

Buck said, "No coward. Jest wants his choice of weapons, a man might say. I'll have to kill him the next time we meet, I reckon."

"He gun for you."

Buck said, "Pick up his cutter. Well, we're a rifle and a short-gun ahead, anyway. Hey, more company."

This time the rider came out of the low foothills. The rider was big and wide and rode bareback. Buck could hardly believe his eyes, for the rider was plainly a woman. When she got closer he saw it was a squaw. He remembered Sandra saying that Big Bob Williams' squaw had been looking for Tortilla Joe.

"More trouble," Buck murmured.

"All the times the more troubles."

The squaw said, "You Tortilla Joe an' you Buck McKee. I look for you. I Many Feathers, Big Bob's squaw. Matt, he kick me out."

Buck said, "Where do we come in?"

"You fight Matt. Me, I fight Matt, too. We join together. The three of us. We kill Matt."

Buck looked at Tortilla Joe, who shrugged.

"Maybe we don't fight him," Buck ventured.

"You two no run. You fight Cross in Circle men last night. You win an' you stay here. You fight." She shook her head. She had her mind made up. Only death could change it. "I stay with you."

Buck tried to change her mind. Many Feathers merely shook her head until her dark braids rattled. "I stay with you mens. You two my mens now."

Buck gave up.

Buck said, "Give her the rifle and the shortgun. Whether we like it or not we got a partner, Tortilla Joe."

He had expected relief to flood the stolid wide face. Still, Many Feathers' face showed nothing. She looked at Buck's swollen face.

"We both got hurts. You win your fight; I lose mine. Maybe I win the last one, though."

"You never win the last one," Buck philosophized. "Death always wins, woman."

TWELVE

When they rode into the yard Sandra Smith nodded at Many Feathers. "See you found them." She looked at Buck. "I knew you'd be back."

"How did you know?"

"You're the type who won't run from danger."

Buck smiled at her. "Thanks for knowing."

Sandra blushed and then Pete Smith came out of the barn and said heartily, "By Gawd, McKee and his pardner. Couldn't make it out of the basin, eh?"

Sandra spoke sternly. "Father, they wouldn't run from Matt Williams, and you know that!"

Buck said, "Williams and his men left town in a group last night. Later on we saw flames from over the ridge."

"They burned down young Paul Hammond's spread. They didn't kill him, though — anyway, we couldn't find the body in the

ashes. Paul was a single man. They're takin'
the single ones first, 'pears to me — warnin'
us with dependants to scoot outa the basin."

"Couldn't find a body, eh?" Buck looked
at Tortilla Joe. "We never heard nothin' in
town about Hammond gettin' in there."

Buck scowled. "Mebbe his body was completely burned?"

"No trace of his carcass," Pete Smith said.
Sandra wiped her eyes.

"I liked Paul," she said. "He had a girl back
in Ohio who he was going to marry. I'll have
to write to her."

Buck wondered just where all this trouble
was going to end. Then he realized he already
knew that answer. He turned his bronc.

"Where are you going, Buck?" Sandra
wanted to know.

"We're not married," Buck reminded her.

Her eyes flashed anger. "No, and we won't
ever be, I can assure you of that!"

Tortilla Joe said, "We take up the homesteads, peoples."

Pete Smith rubbed his bony hands together
and showed a wide smile. Sandra was a little
surprised. Many Feathers merely nodded as
if this were information she had known for
a long time.

"Homesteads! That's good news." Pete
Smith was beaming. "Now us nesters really

95

have a couple of leaders. We need gunsling-
ers —"

Buck said, "Let's get this clear, Smith.
We're not fightin' for you farmers, savvy? We
got a score to settle with Matt Williams. It's
our score, not yours."

"Then you two ain't gonna lead us?"

"We are not."

Sandra said, "Can you blame them, Dad?
They don't even know the rest of the farmers.
The only ones they have met is us."

"That's right," Buck said. "We know one
other, though, Miss Sandra — and I refer to
our good friend, John Powers." The sarcasm
was evident.

They turned their broncs. Many Feathers
also turned her nag. Tortilla Joe said, "You
stay here, squaw."

"I take homestead too maybe no?"

Buck said, "A redskin can't file on land."

Many Feathers' deep eyes twinkled. "I fight
that out with man in town," she said. Whether
or not they wanted her was irrelevant to Many
Feathers. She was staying with them. Her
logic was simple. Matt Williams was their
enemy. Sooner or later they would tangle with
Williams and his crew. When this happened
she wanted to be on hand.

They rode toward Paul Hammond's cabin.
They would file on homesteads and thereby

further incite Matt Williams' hatred toward them. Ag Keller would tell his boss that Buck had downed the gent named Tony.

They came to the ashes of Hammond's shack. A farmer was looking at the ruins. He introduced himself and he seemed to know who they were. Buck and Tortilla Joe looked through the ruins carefully. No body had been burned.

"You look in the brush, farmer?"

"We looked good, McKee."

Buck said, "Any open land for homesteadin' around here?"

The farmer said, "See John Powers. He'll locate you boys."

"Powers won't locate me," Buck grunted. "We're takin' up homesteads. How about that land next to this homestead down the crick a-ways?"

"Free land."

"How do you take up the homesteads?" Tortilla Joe wanted to know.

The farmer explained. You paid a filing fee with the land-agent, who was the Ringbone postmaster. Then you located your homestead on his map. You drove in temporary corner-stakes and later on the surveyor would come out from the county seat and make a legal survey.

"I got a hatchet tied to my saddle," the

farmer said. "You can use it to cut an' drive stakes."

With the help of the farmer they got two homesteads staked out. Both would be one hundred and sixty acres, the legal limit. Buck kept thinking about Paul Hammond.

"Hammond, he no burn," said Many Feathers.

"How do you know?"

"I see blood. Trail go into hills. I find him."

She had been riding along the foothills. The wind during the night had whipped away footprints or hoofprints. Buck would never have noticed the drop of dried blood in the brush.

"Him go that way."

They had sent the farmer home, after returning his hatchet. Buck and Tortilla rode behind Many Feathers, who, many times, had to dismount to further decipher the trail.

They worked for hours. The sun heeled over the zenith had started its downward fall. At last, they found the farmer in the deep buckbrush. He was unconscious. Buck, at first, thought he was dead: he lay so still against the soil. But when he opened the man's shirt he found that his heart still beat.

"He no know nothin'," Many Feathers said.

"We got to get him to the doc. There's a medico in town, ain't there, Many Feathers?"

"One there. Him drunk all the time. Him no good. I doctor heem."

Buck looked down at the wounded youth. Not more than twenty-two, with a thin face and a slender body. A bullet had gone through Hammond's chest high on the right side. He had lost lots of blood and shock had knocked him cold; besides, he had walked about four miles after being shot.

"Where will we take him, Many Feathers?"

"Take him to Smith farm, maybe?"

Tortilla Joe said, "I'll ride ahead. They can meet us at the edge of the hills with a buckboard."

Many Feathers got some grass, wadded it, and blocked the rifle-holes in Hammond's shoulder. Buck poured water from a canteen over the youth's face. His lips moved, his tongue came out; his eyes opened.

"I'm Buck McKee, Hammond. Your friend."

Hammond looked at him almost vacantly. Then his eyes shuttled over to the squaw. "Many Feathers," he murmured. "Big Bob's woman."

"I help you, white mans."

Hammond made a weak smile. He closed his eyes and his lips, said, "God, we need Your help against a terrible enemy. God, help us

99

to be strong, and to win; our side, God, is just."

Many Feathers tore Hammond's bloody shirt into strips. Buck held the limp body upright while she made her bandages. Once their fingers touched. Buck got the impression that she was good and kind and her heart bled for this wounded youth. He figured this Crow squaw had been the best wife Big Bob had ever had.

"Now we can move him, Buck."

Hammond was boosted in front of the squaw, with Buck lifting him onto the old horse. Movement brought some strength to the youth and he dug into the bronc's mane for leverage.

"They came out of the night, I was in the brush —"

Buck murmured, "Hush, fella. Get well first, and then think of other things. Now we'll take you to the Smith farm."

They came out of the hills — a slow-moving pair of riders — and when they reached the rim of the rough country Tortilla Joe and Sandra and Pete Smith awaited with a buckboard. Sandra had put a bunch of grass and a blanket on the floor and they got the youth on this.

At the Smith ranch they got young Hammond into a bed. Sandra and Many Feathers changed his bandages and Many Feathers had the girl kill a chicken so she could make broth. Buck and Tortilla Joe talked with Pete Smith about their new homesteads.

"You'd best file on them soon, eh?"

"We're headin' into town now," Buck said. "Wish we had some fresh horseflesh under our kaks, though."

"I got a couple of broncs. Not fast ones, but fresh."

Buck said, "Thanks, friend."

Many Feathers said, "I stay here. I nurse sick man."

Buck took her worn, heavy hand. "That is good, mother," he said simply. "This ugly world needs more good people like you."

Her eyes glowed.

THIRTEEN

The postmaster was a heavy-set, stolid man of slow movements. He studied Buck and the Mexican as though they were men from another planet.

"Am I hearin' right?" he asked.

Buck said, "You heard right, bucko. We got homesteads staked out and we want to pay filin' fees an' get our applications on record."

"You two is cowpunchers, ain't you?"

"We were," Buck said. "Now, mister, trot out your papers, and we'll pay and sign."

Still, the postmaster made no move — he just stood across the desk, studying them.

Tortilla Joe glanced at Buck. "Maybe he ees the Weeliams man, no, an' he no want us een thees countries?"

Unknowingly the Mexican had spoken the truth. Big Bob Williams had got the postmaster job for this fellow.

"You men don't want homesteads," the

102

postmaster said. "You're cowpunchers, not sodbusters. This is just a passing whim with you. I can't cater to whims and therefore I can't sign you to homesteads."

"You work for the gover'ment, don't you?" Buck asked.

"I do."

"Then you work for me," the cowpuncher said. "Trot out those papers and get this thing lined up in a legal manner, and make it pronto."

Buck was tired and disgusted. Since his arrival on Ringbone grass he had been tricked, had had to fight with his fists, and had killed a man he had not even known. He had not had a pleasant time. Everywhere he turned he met opposition. Even this political hireling of the Cross in a Circle spread was bucking him. . . .

The postmaster was a big man. He had spent a year in the army before he had acquired a "sore" back. He had done some fighting and drinking while there and he imagined himself to be pretty tough. He had picked his opponents rather carefully. He figured he had acquired a rep as a tough man with his fists. Buck McKee had a black eye and his face was swollen from John Powers' fists. The postmaster did not figure Powers as much of a fighter. Therefore his logic ran in this manner:

103

If John Powers could scar up McKee, then *he* could surely whip McKee. So he turned his back and said, "Get the hell outa my office, both of you!"

Buck didn't hit him.

Buck shoved the table forward with a fast savage motion. The edge of it caught the man across his hips and sent him lurching ahead. He ran into the wall, turned, and ran into a right fist. He sat down and his eyes were glazed.

He stared up at Buck McKee. "You —"

Buck pulled him upright. It was a feat of some strength. He tore the postmaster's shirt.

The postmaster hit him and Buck stepped to one side and clipped the man with a left.

When the postmaster came to he was in a chair slumped over the table. Tortilla Joe was at the postal window looking for a letter for the town drunk who had wide eyes.

Buck drew his .45. The postmaster watched with alarmed eyes. Buck walked over to him, pistol dangling. The postmaster, wide awake now, leaned back and his eyes were distended, the pupils wide.

"What you aim to do, McKee?"

Buck gingerly laid the barrel of the gun across the man's thick neck. Apparently he seemed to be selecting a spot on which to hit the man.

"Mister, I'm tired of foolin' aroun', savvy?"

"Matt Williams told me not to let no more homesteads go out of this office. Matt'll kill me —"

"If he doesn't, I will. Now where are the forms?"

"In that second drawer."

"I get them, Bucks," Tortilla said. Buck jugged his .45 into holster. Tortilla Joe came with the forms. The postmaster wet his lips and wanted a drink. He had four bits in a desk drawer. Would Tortilla Joe hurry over to a saloon and get some Old Horseshoe? Tortilla Joe did, and by this time the entire town was in the postoffice watching them. The town drunk evidently was the town's walking newspaper.

"Look at 'em, men!"

One woman said, "I hope they straighten that stupid ox out for good!"

"He's a Williams' man, and don't talk that way."

"Williams is goin' to lose. He can't win."

Buck listened with half an ear. One thing was certain — word of this would get to Matt Williams and get there fast. He noticed a heavy-set man in the crowd — evidently a businessman of some sort. He seemed lazily interested in this, but back of his small grey eyes lurked curiosity. His eyes met Buck's and for a moment each studied the other. Buck became aware of a feeling that this man was studying him the way a man studies an opponent. Maybe this gent was also a Williams' man?

Later, Buck discovered that the man's name was Jacob Mudd. . . .

The postmaster worked silently, filling out the claim-sheets. Gradually the crowd broke up and dispersed. They had come to see a fight. By the time they had got to the postoffice the postmaster had been a tamed tomcat. Outside, a rider sped past the postoffice, heading out of town at a hard lope; his hoof sounds died.

Tortilla Joe said, "He rode a Cross een a Circle hoss, Buck."

"A spy, goin' to report to Matt Williams." Buck returned his attention to the postmaster. "That's right, fella. Well, those two claims are filed; what's the fee?"

"Twenty bucks."

"For both?"

"No, for one filin' claim. That makes forty for both."

Buck shook his head. "The farmers told me the fee was two dollars per claim. Seems to me you raised the ante a little on us, and why?"

"The farmers told you wrong. The fee for both of you is forty bucks. Pay up or I won't

106

put my signature on this."

Buck shook his head in feigned sadness. He didn't have twenty bucks and Tortilla Joe did not have that much either. But there was no use telling this man that they were broke.

"Put your John Hancock on that," he ordered.

"Not unless you pay me."

Buck put his .45 behind the postmaster's left ear. The postmaster winced.

Buck said, "That gun barrel too cold for you? I could warm it a little and then put it back under your ear."

"When you pulls the treeger," Tortilla Joe said, "the barrel she get warm, Buck."

Buck cocked the big gun. The sound was loud in the silent room.

The postmaster signed. Buck put his gun away. The postmaster said, "This was under duress, men."

Carefully, Buck put the document in his pocket. "Duress?" He feigned ignorance. "Heck, I don't even know what that word means."

FOURTEEN

The man named Jacob Mudd had kept his mouth shut and his ears open and inside of a few hours he had had the lay of the land clearly in his mind.

He talked, nodded, seemed agreeable; yet, back of his small eyes, ran his thoughts. They were evil thoughts, motivated by greed. John Powers was working his scheme correctly. He was pitting the farmers against the Williams' riders, and the farmers would lose — and Powers would be the winner because, with the farmers gone, Powers would own their lands, and then Powers and a man named Jacob Mudd would be rich.

There was a fly in the ointment — two flies, in fact. He had determined that fact almost immediately. One fly was named Buck Mc-Kee. The other — a fat ugly fly — was named Tortilla Joe.

John Powers, he realized, had made one great mistake when he had lured Buck Mc-

Kee and Tortilla Joe onto Ringbone range —
and his nefarious scheme to use their gun
speeds had backfired on him. Now the farmers
were flocking around McKee and the Mexican.

Mudd's appraisal had been accurate. McKee
was nobody's fool. Tortilla Joe was no fool
because he travelled with McKee, and McKee
made the tough decisions.

They were two tough enemies.

Jacob Mudd had rolled his cigar between
his red lips and had gone to the livery barn
where he had rented a horse. He would use
it when darkness came. He spent the rest of
the day moving from saloon to saloon, from
the hotel lobby through the stores, and he
talked a little and he listened much. A man
in the Star Rowel Saloon had openly vowed
he would kill both Buck McKee and his partner. The man's nose was swollen somewhat.

Jacob Mudd made some discreet inquiries.
The man's name, he found out, was Ag Keller,
and Keller rode for the Williams' Cross in a
Circle spread.

"You a farmer?" Keller had demanded suddenly.

Jacob Mudd had stood at the bar turning
his bottle of beer and making damp rings on
the glossy surface.

"Mister, are you a farmer?"

Jacob Mudd acted surprised. "You speaking to me, sir?"

"Yeah, to you. Are you going out farming?"

Jacob Mudd's voice was placating. "Do I look that stupid, sir? If I do, perhaps a drink for both of us will help us overlook my stupidity? Barkeeper, another beer for me, and whatever the man desires for himself."

"You sound like a good fella," Keller mumbled, the wind taken out of his sails. "Here's to you, mister."

"To you also, sir."

Keller wiped his mouth with his hand. "I'm goin' to kill them two buttons sure as Gawd made green apples."

"There they ride out now."

Ag Keller turned, hooked his elbows back over the rim of the bar, and watched Buck and Tortilla Joe ride out of town.

As they went out of sight, Jacob Mudd spoke to the bartender. "Reckon them two boys have really raised hell in this burg, eh?"

"A little bit," the bartender replied. "I think they can raise more though. They don't look a bit soft to me. That Mex shot down Sig Rudder kinda easy like, and Rudder had a rep as a gunhand."

"Slow hand he had," Ag Keller scoffed. "I could shoot him down any day of the week."

Jacob Mudd left to wander around town again, loafing with ears alert.

When darkness came he went to the livery barn. He saddled the hired horse and rode toward John Powers' homestead. He rode well, settling his bulk deep between the fork and cantle.

Apparently he was in no hurry, for he never got the horse out of a trot. It was a large, fine night. Coolness had come to push away the heat of the day. Along Ringbone Creek wild roses bloomed and sent out their perfume. A trout jumped.

He followed the creek, and when he came to the yard of John Powers' homestead he called, "Rider coming in, John." The house had a lamp lit in it and this spilled its rays across the dusty yard. Nobody answered and a vague resentment arose in Jacob Mudd.

He controlled this and again called, "Visitor, John Powers. Peaceful man."

Behind him he heard a boot strike rock. He looked over his shoulder and saw a man coming out of the buckbrush about a hundred feet away.

"That you, Jacob?"

"Who the hell else you expecting?" Mudd made his voice a grating rasp. "You know my voice, don't you?"

"I figured it was you but I weren't sure.

A man has got to be sure on this range."

"Would an enemy ride openly into your yard?"

"A man can't tell what dirty trick Matt Williams will use. Light an' rest your stirrups, Jacob."

They went into the house with Powers leading the way, with Jacob Mudd waddling behind. Once in the house Powers said, "Find a chair somewhere, Jacob."

Mudd looked around, eyes speculative. "McKee and you sure busted up the furniture."

"We sure did."

Mudd decided on the bunk. Once settled, he leaned forward, chubby hands clasped between his thick knees.

"Didn't expect you here for some weeks yet," Powers said.

Mudd cleared his throat. "John, this is going too slowly. We got to get these deeds right pronto. The big company I represent is getting restless. They want these deeds and they want this tin mined and out of here."

"I'm doin' my best."

"You got deeds of about three homesteaders, I understand. We need more deeds. We can't go in on government land and mine because the government won't let us. Uncle Sam wants tin, too."

"I hope," said John Powers, "that there *is* tin here."

"It's here. I'm a geologist. I've scouted this land. Only thing we have to do is to get these deeds and strike while this big corporation is interested. They're scouting for tin in Peru and Colombia, too. We got to beat those geologists to it."

"I'm doin' my best."

"I disagree with you."

Anger rolled a ruddy path across John Powers' ugly swollen face. "Don't rub my fur the wrong direction, Mudd. I'll do to you what I did that day in the prison yard down in Yuma."

"Forget that prison deal!"

"We're both ex-jailbirds, and don't forget it. I went over the wall and you stuck your sentence out. Just because I'm wanted in Arizona Territory — well, don't try to hold that over my head, savvy?"

"I served my sentence. Three years for oil fraud, and I never made a damned cent out of it, either. But there's a hell of a difference between fraud and murder, especially when a woman is the one murdered."

"She asked for it. She doublecrossed me."

Jacob Mudd waved his cigar impatiently. "We're talking like kids. Our past has nothing to do with the present outside of the fact that

113

we met in Yuma. I still claim you haven't made things move fast enough."

"I'm working the nesters against the Cross in a Circle. I'm pushin' Williams hard. We had a stroke of luck when Big Bob died. Matt is hitting harder than his father did. He's burned two shacks in a couple of nights. The fear of the future is with these farmers."

Jacob Mudd shook his head again. "Sure, you pitted the farmers against Williams, but what else have you done?"

"All right, if you're so damn smart, do some talkin'!"

Mudd rolled his cigar. "I understand this Williams has a girl down town. Now if some farmer — say yourself — could get her away from Matt Williams!"

"That's out."

"Why?"

"She sold out and she left town today. Mildred James is out of the picture."

Mudd studied him through tawny eyes. He took his cigar down and studied it thoughtfully. "John, we got to speed things up. You made a hell of an error when you got this McKee gent in here. Him and that Mex are tough enemies."

"Yes, I made an error there. Didn't you ever make one?"

Again Mudd smiled. "Yes, on that oil stock

deal, and it put me behind bars in Yuma. . . . You miss one point, though."

"And that?"

"You personally haven't hit at the Cross in a Circle. You've hit at Williams indirectly so far."

"That's right."

"You and I are going to hit directly at him with a blow he can blame on your farmers, and then Williams will hit back fast."

"That's logic."

Mudd lifted his dull eyes from his cigar. "We can burn down some property. Property belonging to the Cross in a Circle."

Their eyes met. Mudd's scheming, dull, filled with devilish wisdom; the swollen, bright eyes of John Powers. Then Mudd got to his feet, throwing his cigar out the door.

"Let's ride, John," the man murmured.

FIFTEEN

Spur rowels gouged into the varnished surface of the big table in the living room of the Cross in a Circle ranch house. The spurs were hooked onto polished boots. The man wore pants with a knife-crease, and his belt was wide with a silver buckle. You saw a clean black shirt, a bow tie, and then you saw the face of young Matt Williams, a wide handsome face, flushed with whiskey; a young face, strangely hard-looking for its few years.

You could see that the squaw had gone. The room, usually clean and spotless, was dirty with litter, and now the air was gray with rope-like tobacco smoke. Matt Williams lit another cigar.

A rider came along the creek, and the new owner of the Cross in a Circle listened to the pound of hoofs, and thereby judged the rider's speed — and he rode fast. He drew rein and clumped into the house. It was one of Matt's riders.

116

"Jus' come from town, Matt. Them two hellions beat up on the postmaster and made him draw up forms for them."

"Forms? For what, Smoky?"

"Homesteads, of course. They got homesteads out along the crick, somewhere aroun' the Smith homestead."

"Are you fillin' me full of hot air, Smoky? They're *cowpunchers,* not homesteaders."

"They're homesteaders now, Matt."

"What else do you know?"

"I reckon they know now they kilt Big Moccasin last night."

"That means nothin'!"

"Well, thet's the deal from town, boss." The cowpuncher got to his feet. "Thet big postmaster shore had a pale lookin' face when McKee had his gun behin' his ear!"

Matt Williams was remembering, suddenly, that Mildred James had left him, and, for a moment, he had a pang of regret.

"Get back to town, Smoky!"

"I need money for chuck at the café, Matt."

Matt smiled. "You got credit there. Now get on your nag and head back. Kill McKee or the Mex and it's a hundred bucks for each's hide. Bump off the postmaster and it's fifty bucks for your purse."

Idly Matt Williams listened to the man's boots run out, and then he heard the rider

117

turn his bronc. Through the front window he watched Smoky ride to the barn and saddle a fresh horse and head out of town. Again, he was thinking of Mildred James — she was gone, he would never see her again. With this was a harsh feeling of loss. And he lowered his head to the table and, for a moment, he almost wept. But reality and greed came back and pushed into limbo the emotion of love.

He was sitting there in the dark living room, at dusk, when Ag Keller entered. Keller peered around the room, said, "Matt, you in here?" He came forward and sat down and locked his hands in front of him and looked at them. "McKee and the Mex took up homesteads today."

"Smoky told me."

Keller looked up. "Oh, yes? I saw him ride past the postoffice when McKee and his pard were workin' over the fat postmaster. I rode past McKee's homestead, and four farmers were there, families and all, waitin' for him an' the Mex."

"Waiting?"

"Yeah, he's their leader, now."

"McKee don't like them sodbusters. He just took up that homestead so he'd pull us into hitting at him. He's nobody's fool. He wants trouble because of last night."

"He killed Big Moccasin."

"Good riddance."

"McKee was talkin' to them farmers. I met Joe out in the hills after McKee an' the Mex left town. Joe said McKee and the Mex rode for their new homesteads and the farmers was there a-waitin' them."

"McKee is only a man. So is the Mex. You sound like they're supernatural. Hell, one bullet in the right place will kill each of them! You brag of your gun. Move it against them and get them out of the way!"

Keller said, "This squaw — this Many Feathers. . . . I don't like her bein' around. She'll kill and not blink a red eye."

"She's a minor point, too. If you can't talk sense, get t'hell outa here and leave me alone."

Keller stood up. "You're in a rough mood, Matt."

"You tangled with McKee today. He worked you over a little with his fists. From what I hear you didn't make much of a showing!"

Keller studied him. "How did you know?"

"I got spies in the hills. One watched you."

Keller said, "There'll be another time."

"There'd better be. And it had best be *your* time, fellow, or else I'm sendin' you down the road, talkin' to yourself!"

"I might ride off this job."

Williams scoffed, "No, you won't. You got it too easy and your wages are too high. Go to the bunkhouse and tell the boys to get ready to ride inside of an hour."

Keller turned and went to the bunkhouse.

He felt angry and hot and he wished he could kill Buck McKee. The Big Boss was raw under the collar. Well, Mildred James had left him; that was one reason. McKee and the Mex was another. Another was the farmers.

Men lay on bunks and read magazines and some cleaned gear and boots and three were at the far end of the long room playing cards at a rickety table. Keller knew these men had heard about his run-in with Buck McKee. His prestige had taken a severe tumble. McKee would pay for it. Only by killing Buck McKee could he get his prestige back.

"We ride inside an hour, men."

A man asked, "We hit at McKee?"

"I dunno. Matt didn't say where we hit."

"McKee is laughin' at this spread. You're supposed to be the top tough boy on the Williams' payroll. From what I hear McKee pulled the old rooster's tail feathers danged easy."

Keller turned, walked over, and slapped the man across the mouth so hard blood showed. Keller drew his .45 and the man's hand stopped halfway toward his gun.

"You try to pull this rooster's tail feathers, Jim?"

The man looked at him. He looked at the gun. He said, "You're too much for me, Ag. Put the peashooter away." The man got a magazine and gave his attention to his reading material. Keller grinned and holstered his gun. "Anybody else feel spry against Ag Keller on this fine Wyomin' evenin'?"

A thick chested man said, sourly, "Save it for later on, you two. You might need it tonight."

Keller took down his .45 and cleaned it and then methodically cleaned his rifle. He checked each weapon for loads. By this time darkness had rushed down from the Big Horns.

Matt Williams came in, carrying a Winchester. "All right, men, get your broncs," he ordered, and turned toward the barn. They followed him into the barn's interior and under the light of the lantern hanging from the ridge beam they selected their horses. Saddles lifted and cinches were tied and rifles slid into saddle boots.

They led their broncs outside and boots found stirrups. Williams rode a black gelding and his men rode dark horses — blacks and sorrels and blue roans and dark bays. He gave orders in a low voice.

Somebody said, "We leave a guard behind, don't we, Matt?"

"Yeah, a guard stays behind." Williams looked them over, letting his gaze move from man to man. "Are there any questions?"

There was none.

They sped out of the yard, a compact body of hard-riding men sweeping across the moonlit Wyoming prairie. Matt Williams headed them, letting the black run with a fierce swiftness. He looked at the moon, and he thought of Mildred James' golden hair.

Again, the feeling of deep loss came. . . . Even a desperate man, bent on hate and death, could remember love . . . could recall tenderness. . . . Matt cursed quietly.

SIXTEEN

Buck McKee and Tortilla Joe left the town of Ringbone after receiving copies of their filing papers from the clerk. An axe was tied to Buck's saddle, also a gunny-sack that bulged with canned goods and other commodities. Tortilla Joe jogged along, a sack of nails tied to one side of his saddle; on the other side, he had a skillet and a pot.

His bronc, tired as he was, did not like the skillet and pot; they bounced and hit him on the ribs, making him skittish.

"That postmaster — *hola,* Buck, but we feex heem, no?"

"He don't love us," Buck said.

Tortilla Joe sent his partner a quick sidewise glance. "You do not sound so happy."

Buck spat and grinned. "Who could be happy? We're in trouble. Williams is out to get us more than ever now. So is Ag Keller. Keller ain't forgettin' that pushin' around I handed him. Now Williams will be after us for sure, just to make an example out of us."

"He have the hard time. Me, I no like to be made the goat, and that ees what we ees now, *no es verdad?*"

"We put ourselves on the spot."

Tortilla Joe untied a *tortilla* and put his white teeth noisily into it. "Shore, we does that, pard. But theenk of Mees Sandra Smeeth."

"I don't want to think of her. I might get to like her too well, and then I'd think of her so much I'd want her close."

Buck rode an easy saddle — a lazy saddle — but he was deceptively lazy, loafing between horn and cantle. Sandra Smith was a nice girl, a clean sweet girl, but there were other girls, too, just as sweet, just as clean, just as good. Maybe Tortilla Joe was right? Perhaps he was bucking the Cross in a Circle combine because of Sandra? Was he fooling himself, and fooling nobody else, when he swore vengeance on John Powers, and on Matt Williams?

Tortilla swallowed the last of the *tortilla*. "My throat she ees dry. Now if only I had a dreenk."

Buck was thinking of John Powers, and he realized that Powers was a hard enemy. What stake did the man have in this basin? Sure, he had located some of the farmers on their homesteads, deriving from this fact a few dollars. He was sure that John Powers had some other reason for attempting to wrestle Ringbone range from the Cross in a Circle. He did not know what that reason was. Had he this information, this knowledge, his course of action would become more stable.

But he had no way of finding out. Accordingly his mind went over to the Cross in a Circle. Matt Williams would see that he and Tortilla Joe had plenty of trouble. By signing up for homesteads, they had run against the grain of Matt Williams. They had waved a red flag in his face. One thought bothered Buck — where would Williams hit next?

This was, to put it mildly, rather complicated. Even the squaw, Many Feathers, was in on it. In her narrowed, deep eyes glowed a fanatical light — the light of a person obsessed with one paramount idea. By all rights she should have had a share of the Cross in a Circle after the passing of Big Bob Williams. Her share, though, had been a boot in the face.

He and Tortilla Joe had moved against the Cross in a Circle, against John Powers, to satisfy themselves, not to aid the farmers. Of course, they were all banded together in this, but necessity had put them together, not deliberate choice.

Tortilla Joe's voice broke into his thoughts.

"That fat mans down een town," Tortilla Joe said, watching Buck. "He put the beeg nose of hees aroun' an' first he sneef thees way, then he sneef thees way. He smell around like he ees a dog."

"Jacob Mudd is his name."

"How you find out?"

"I asked a few questions and did some lookin' around myself. Wonder what he aims to do on this range?"

Tortilla Joe shrugged, heavy shoulders lifting, then falling.

Buck said, "I'm keepin' an eye on him."

Buck and Tortilla rode into the yard of the Smith farm. Once again, Sandra was feeding her chickens.

She showed a nice smile. "I'm always feeding chickens when you boys ride in. I heard you two have taken up homesteads?"

"News gets around fast," Buck admitted.

"A farmer was in town when you beat up on the postmaster. For that I want to thank you — he had it coming. Now all the farmers know about you two having farms, too."

Buck dismounted. He asked, "Where is your father?"

"Over at your homestead."

Buck looked at her and his eyebrows rose questioningly. "I don't quite understan' that statement, Miss Sandra. What is your father doing on a piece of ground that's undeveloped?"

"All the farmers are there."

Buck nodded, understanding. "They're gathered there to welcome me an' Tortilla Joe, eh?"

"They are."

Buck said, "Whether we like it or not, Sandra, the farmers have made me an' Tortilla Joe their leaders, eh?"

"That's it. They have always needed a leader. They thought they had one in John Powers. Most of them by now have lost faith in Powers. They had automatically selected you two as their leaders."

Buck spoke in a cynical manner. "That shore is nice, Miss Sandra. But what if we don't want to be their leaders? When it comes to a showdown we'll have to run against the Williams' spread. I don't think those sodmen would be worth a whoop in hell when the lead starts flyin'."

"You settle that with them," she said.

Her tone had suddenly grown almost frigid. Evidently, then, when a person said something about the other farmers, she took it as an almost personal insult. This group, Buck realized, was very tightly knitted together. Perhaps he had underestimated the courage and the strength of these sodbusters. Sandra had lots of spunk and scrap. If they were anything like she was, then they would be good hands to have siding a man in a tight fight.

"How is Hammond?"

"He seems to be well." She was too icy again.

"On what do you base that statement?"

"I was sitting by his bed, feeling sorry for him. He tried to get his arm around me!"

Buck winked at Tortilla Joe. "I don't blame him, Sandra. Was I in bed where he is, I'd try to get my arm around you, too."

"Oh, you would, would you!"

They went into the cabin.

Dusk filled the cabin, making vision uncertain; Buck saw the huge outline of Many Feathers, sitting on a chair beside the bed.

Hammond said, "Howdy, men. Again, I want to thank you."

"How do you feel, bucko?"

Hammond sounded as though he were in a weakened condition, but he sounded cheerful. He would get better now. He had lost all his property, and he had almost lost his life. Night-riders had cleaned him out. His voice held a harsh edge of hate that was directed toward nobody else than Matt Williams.

"And I didn't get a one of them. I was asleep

in my cabin when they rode in. . . ."

Buck said, "We'll see you later, Hammond," and he and Tortilla Joe went outside, with Many Feathers trailing them, her dress rustling.

"You two mens, you have the homesteads now?"

"Farmers now," Buck agreed.

Her dark, Crow eyes moved from one to the other. "Matt Williams will fight you now for sure. But he is not as big an enemy as John Powers."

Buck said, "How do you know?"

Buck saw her tongue come out and wet her lips. Her big-knuckled hands gripped the looseness of her baggy dress and twisted the cloth.

"He has bad eyes. He has the eyes of a bad, bad bronc."

Then she turned, moving quickly despite her size, and was gone. Buck looked at Tortilla Joe who said, "Sometimes, there ees such a theeng as instinct, or whatever you calls eet."

Buck said, "You said it, pard."

SEVENTEEN

Buck and Tortilla Joe rode down Ringbone Creek, following a trail that ran along the south bank of the stream. It was almost dark when they rode around the bend in the hills and came upon their homesteads.

The farmers were awaiting them.

Some had ridden in on horses, others had come by rigs. They made a good sized gathering. Whether they liked it or not, it looked to Buck as if the farmers had chosen him and Tortilla Joe as their leaders. Things had happened fast on this Ringbone range. Here he was, the appointed leader of the farmers, and he had not even met some of them as yet!

In a way, it was amusing; from another angle, it was a grim business.

Tortilla Joe said, "About ten of them, no?"

Buck sent a quick glance over the buggies, buckboards, wagons and saddle horses, and nodded. "About a dozen, I'd say. Took their women and kids along, even."

A cheer went up from the assembled people. Kids ran out to meet Buck and Tortilla, and Buck had to warn them to stay a careful distance away from their saddle horses.

Buck and his partner reached the parents, and these people were not excited. They were calm and grim and an air of tension held them.

Buck dismounted, and Tortilla Joe followed suit. Pete Smith stepped out of the crowd, a thin unshaven man bent by his years — a homely man with a crooked nose, but a sincere and good man.

"Neighbors McKee and Tortilla Joe, we thought we would welcome you to our ranks, so we made this little gathering, and we hope you like it. We have food and we shall eat some, and maybe later on we will dance."

Buck felt the sincerity of the occasion grip him, and he had difficulty speaking. Tortilla Joe nodded vigorously, his smile wide and happy.

Buck said, "I want to thank you, Mister Smith; I want to thank you all. It is good to have good neighbors but we must remember we are all under stress, and under danger."

"Maybe," a man said, "we should forget danger for a while? It's not good to always bend under one's troubles." Farmers flocked around, introducing themselves. Women curtsied and smiled and children ran and played. Soon baskets of food came from rigs and tablecloths were spread on the grass. Buck knew, now, that he and Tortilla Joe were the leaders of these people, whether he and his partner wanted or did not want the job.

Buck searched for the reason he had not his usual high taste for good food, for this food was indeed good. Pickles and luscious sandwiches, pots of boiling coffee, relish and canned goods. He decided, after some deliberation, that his appetite suffered because of the predicament he was in, and he wondered if he feared for the safety of these people. That thought, coming suddenly to him, was almost alarming.

Tortilla Joe, seated some distance away, ate with other farmers, and Buck heard him laugh occasionally. His meal finished, Buck thanked his hostess — a heavyset woman who had a daughter of about seventeen — and got to his feet. Instantly the girl was beside him.

"Would you like to walk around, Mr. McKee?"

She was just filling out in maturity, and Buck liked her pretty young face. "With your company, Miss Betty, the walk would be more fun."

Her mother said, "Betty, show Mr. McKee

around, while I clean up things. We had all best get home. Our homes are unprotected."

He walked around the gathering, with Betty chattering beside him. Only three of the farmers had wives here; others, so Betty said, were married, but their families were in the midwest and east, and would come to Ringbone after their husbands and fathers had become settled.

Buck wondered why Betty had suddenly decided to spend her time on him. He was much older than she. He got the idea, for some reason, that she had seen, in him, an excuse to get away from her mother's possessive apron strings.

Buck saw her wink at a youth of about twenty — a gangling boy who had introduced himself as Sid Latham, a son of a farmer named Mike Latham. Betty wanted to talk to the youth.

Therefore Buck, to be obliging, talked with Sid's father, a short man with long arms. Mike Latham was in favor of storming the Williams' ranch. Here Matt Williams had burned down two farmers' outfits, had killed Jack Maloney, and had shot down Paul Hammond.

The farmer pounded his fists together. "I move we hold a meeting and run our guns against them gunhounds!"

Buck caught the stale odor of whiskey on the man's breath. Somebody had taken some liquor to this meeting, and that was not good. From the corner of his eye he saw Betty talking with young Sid. They were very much in love, Buck guessed, and he remembered his first sweetheart. A man got old too fast; his days ran away with him. He did not want to talk with Latham any longer. The man was getting drunk and when he got drunk he evidently wanted to fight.

Suddenly a fiddle began screeching, an alien sound in the Wyoming hills. Tortilla Joe, always one to dance, grabbed Betty, and they began. Buck stood to one side, talking with various farmers — he was feeling them out, gauging them, testing their desires and mettle. He had been wrong when he had sized this group up as weaklings.

These men were fighters. They had come to Ringbone to settle down, to raise their families, and they were ready to fight for this opportunity. Buck was, in a way, proud to be a leader of their ranks. Then, as he looked at their wives and children, when he thought of the women and children who were not present, he felt serious misgivings. War meant death and death meant weeping women and heartsick children.

Suddenly a big form materialized beside him

and he stood up, doffing his hat automatically.

Betty's mother frowned. "We should go home, Mr. McKee. What if the Williams' crowd struck tonight at a farm house?" she asked. "Our properties are deserted."

"That's right, ma'am."

"I wish I knew where Betty went to."

"She's gone?"

"I can't see her anywhere."

Buck moved through the group, looking for the girl. He was quick to note that Sid Latham was gone, too. Well, it wasn't *his* daughter, nor was Latham his son. He talked with Betty's father, who told him Betty had gone home to do the chores. Buck nodded, told about the mother's anxiety, but did not, of course, mention the fact that young Latham had left, too.

Tortilla Joe seemed to be having a good time. He was swinging the women around, his wide face sporting a dark, wide smile. Buck got him aside and told him teasingly that if Margarita could see him she would cut his throat with her dullest butcher knife.

"She no got strings on me, Buck."

"She'd like to have them."

One man said, "Where the hell is John Powers, the skunk?" He answered his own question. "Got us out here, collected his fee, an' then deserted us."

"Good riddance," Betty's father claimed.

"I say the same," a woman declared.

One man said, "That fat guy that got off the stage — his name is Jacob Mudd. I was back in the hills today, scoutin' aroun', an' I done seen him."

"Where did Mudd go?"

"Rode over to see John Powers, he did."

That silenced them. They looked at each other and wondered. Buck did some thinking, too — did this all tie in in some manner? He remembered how Mudd had looked at him and Tortilla Joe there in the Ringbone post-office after they had manhandled the postmaster. Mudd's heavily lidded eyes had held a silent appraisal. A scheming, appraising look, a look that penetrates, weighs and judges.

"Wonder who he is an' what he wanted with Powers?"

"I dunno, Jones."

Suddenly somebody said, "Hey, look over that way — over toward the hills. There's a house on fire, over there!"

Instantly the fiddle stopped. Dancers stopped in the middle of a step. They all stared toward the east. There, over the rim of a rugged hill, was a red glow against the moonlight — a glow made by a fire.

For a moment, then, silence held the group. Beside Buck stood Betty's mother.

"That's our — home!" she gasped.

Instantly all was confusion. Teams were harnessed to rigs, riders hit for their saddles — horses wheeled, and riders went out, dust rising behind them. And Buck McKee and his partner headed them on the wild night ride.

EIGHTEEN

John Powers said, suddenly, "Riders ahead, Mudd!" And he and the heavy-set man put their broncs into the high buckbrush. They dismounted and went to the heads of their horses and held their hands over the distended nostrils to keep them from whinnying. The hoofs came closer, and John Powers thought, "Quite a few riders," and he waited. Then, they poured around the bend of the hill, moonlight sharp and bright around them, with the dust a fine silver in the moonlight.

John Powers watched.

They passed about a hundred yards away, heading for the east. John Powers got the smell of sweaty horseflesh, and they were gone, then.

"Who was that?" Jacob Mudd asked.

Powers grunted, "Luck is with us, Jacob. That was none other than his Royal Nibs, the Heir Apparent."

"Talk sense," Mudd growled.

"That was Matt Williams and his men! They've left the Cross in a Circle to raise hell with a nester, and now we move in while they are gone."

"They'll have a guard out, don't worry."

Powers wondered where they were going, and who, on this silent night, would be their victim. He remembered how Matt Williams had headed them, a rifle across his saddle, and he remembered the moonlight reflecting from the rifle's barrel.

Things were working out the way he wanted. The nesters, he knew, were on Ringbone Creek, welcoming Buck McKee: while they were there the Cross in a Circle would burn down some more of their property. Well, more power to Matt Williams. Now, after he and Jacob Mudd had accomplished their night's work, Williams would be further incensed against the sodmen.

They climbed a small hill, and, from the height, John Powers looked back to see the Cross in a Circle riders in the distance — moving pinpoints on the breast of the moonlit plain. One rider was some distance ahead of the main body of horsemen, and Powers guessed that impatience was a living, driving force in Matt Williams.

One of the Williams' scouts had come in

to tell him the nesters were on Ringbone Creek.

"Them nesters, they're all on Ringbone Crick, waitin' for Buck McKee. He done took up homesteads today — him an' that Mex pard of his'n."

"I know that."

"Well, Matt, I jest told you. No use to be so hardboiled about it. They're there, an' their shacks is deserted, I'd say."

"Where we headin' for?" a rider wanted to know.

Ag Keller said, "Thet nester at the foot of Eagle Butte. Thet one thet's got thet purty daughter named Betty." He rolled his big eyes. "Lord, is she a beauty. If'n I could ever get both arms around her —"

"What would you do?" challenged Matt Williams.

Keller grinned crookedly, but had no answer. The rest of the Cross in a Circle riders laughed, but the laugh was not healthy. It was the tight laughter of tense men.

"Her father is at the meetin'," the scout informed them. "She's there, too. She's sweet on a punk farmer, ain't she?"

Matt Williams ordered the scout back into the hills to further spy on the farmers. The man turned and rode away without a word, sensing the sternness of the cowman's mood.

Keller decided to play along with Williams. He made the statement that the next time he saw McKee, he intended to shoot him down.

At this information, Matt Williams snorted loudly and said that talk was cheap, but it took money to buy whiskey.

"Hit the trail!" Williams ordered, and turned his bronc on his hind legs, walking him around.

Again, they took to the trail, heading east. They skirted the spot where the farmers were having their celebration and they took to the hills for a shortcut.

The trail narrowed, and the riders were strung out. They threaded their way along the lip of the cliff. Rocks slid and tumbled and landed in the canyon below with the sound of brush being ripped apart, and at one point the trail narrowed dangerously. One horse slipped, slid; his squeal was loud and piercing — a shrill cry of Death. But his rider left the saddle, and, by surging hard against his reins, he jerked the horse back to safety.

Williams rode with reckless abandon. Somehow, he got the impression that this thing was coming to its end. Never did he have any doubt as to the eventual outcome, as to the eventual winner. Always the Cross in a Circle had won. Arrogant, sprawling, the ranch had, since its beginning, lorded it over the rest of the country, and it had run other cow outfits out of the valley — using force, if necessary, to attain its goal.

They left the narrow trail, coming to a mesa that was thick with sagebrush and greasewood as high as the shoulders of a horse. He put his bronc across this, his men trailing him. A horse slid, a rock echoed; then they were again on the grassy plain of Ringbone Valley. And big Matt Williams drew rein, right hand high in a signal for a conference.

His men crowded around him. Men leaned on stirrups and listened, and they took their orders silently.

"The spread is right over the hill. There might be a guard out. We circle on foot, and if there is a guard — kill him like we killed Maloney. Don't let him get out alive like Hammond got out alive.

"All right, men, dismount. Smokey, stay with the broncs. Who's got the can of kerosene?"

"Right here, Matt."

"Good. Bring it along."

Smoky held the reins while men melted into the surrounding brush and the hills. Kerosene gurgled in the can. Williams moved to the south, Ag Keller with him, and they came out of the brush. The homestead shack was below them and to the north a hundred yards.

Keller stopped, peered down at the shack. "What'd you see?"

"Thought mebbe I seen somethin' move down there."

"Nobody there, the scout said."

"He might have made a mistake," Keller grumbled. "Reckon I never saw nobody. Hey, what is that?"

Somebody had darted out of the cabin. A rifle talked and the man stumbled, hitting the ground hard. He rolled over, landed in a heap, and did not move. The sound of the rifle was loud. Mingled with it was the sharp cry of a girl. She ran for the brush, and Keller shot; Williams shot, too. Twin bullets lanced flame into the moonlight. But she ran swiftly, and the brush claimed her.

Keller gasped, "That was Betty! She had a gink in the cabin with her — Who the hell is he?"

"I don't know. He's over there."

"I'll catch her," Keller grunted, and ran into the brush.

Matt Williams thought, "He'll never catch her," and he moved forward. He came to the prone figure and knelt and he turned the man over. He was dead; his heart had been almost ripped from his body; a .30-30 cartridge had

143

done that. His head lopped back and Williams saw that the dead man was in his late teens. He looked up at one of his riders who said, "That's thet farmer's kid — name is Sid Latham. He's dead, eh?"

"Plumb dead."

Matt Williams got to his feet. He wiped his hands carefully on his pants. He said, "Save some for the out-buildings. We burn them, too."

"All right, Matt."

Williams spoke to two riders. "Throw this gent's body into the building."

The body of Sid Latham crashed through the window and hit the floor. A match did its work, and the flames danced up the dried log building. Another match lit the henhouse, then the barn.

Keller came back, puffing like a windbroken horse. "She — she got away, boss. We'd best get outa here pronto!"

"Why?"

Matt Williams' face was lighted by the glow of the fires.

Keller said, "Why? Them farmers'll see this fire, an' they'll come hell-bent for election thisaway —"

"Let 'em come!"

Keller showed a toothy, savage smile. "I can see your point now. This oughta drive the gutless hyenas into action, 'specially with that dead kid in the flames. But we want the fight on our terms, not theirs, don't we?"

A rider came piling down off the hills, his bronc running wildly.

"The Cross in a Circle, Matt! It's on fire!"

"What?"

The guard said, "So help me, Matt, they's a fire at the ranch. A big one, too. Look, you kin see the color ag'in the sky from here!"

They swiveled, and they looked. For a moment nobody spoke. The flames crackled, hens squalled in the burning henhouse, and flames made dancing wild shadows on the parched earth.

"Those dirty farmers!" Matt Williams ground out his words. "They've fired my ranch! There'll be flame and death across this valley tonight! This is the showdown!"

"You said it," Ag Keller affirmed.

NINETEEN

When the guard heard the movement of a man ahead in the brush, he left his hiding place in the shadow of a cottonwood tree and he moved silently ahead, working toward that movement. He never heard the man come in behind him. Suddenly an arm encircled his neck from the rear. The knife rose, came in, found his heart.

Then the guard was falling, his knees bending, and John Powers stood there, legs spread wide, the knife red in his hands. And the lips of John Powers showed a crooked, satanical grin.

"I got him, friend," Powers said quietly.

Jacob Mudd's massive bulk moved closer. "We did it, eh? I made a good decoy, huh?"

"You did all right."

"Might be another guard out."

"There ain't."

"How do you know?"

"I've scouted this outfit for months. This

146

gent was always left behind as a guard. I watched his path for some time now."

"Hope you're right."

"I am right."

They had a coal-oil can tied to a saddle. Mudd got this, and a chuckle came from the cavity of his huge belly — he liked the sound of the liquid gurgling in the can. Already John Powers had moved into the clearing, and he stood there — a man openly defined against the moonlight, clear to the eyes of a possible watcher, had there been one.

Mudd thought, "He's got bravery," and he felt the tremble of fear in his own gross muscles as he moved forward, the grass crunching under his boots.

"Where at first?"

Calmly, John Powers stood there, looking at the immense ranch. He wet his thumb and tested the direction of the wind.

Evidently this direction pleased him. He smiled. "The bunkhouse first. Then the flames will sweep to the house, if this wind holds its velocity and direction."

"I don't like standing out here in the open," Mudd said, and his voice was not too calm.

Powers said, "There's an old hostler on the ranch, but he's asleep in the haymow of the barn."

"There is? He might come awake —"

"He sleeps sound."

Powers went across the clearing. From behind the house came the sudden wild barking of the hounds in their pens. Evidently they had just smelled the intruders. For a moment Powers thought the fat man would run.

"They're in pens, Mudd."

"For Gawd's sake, don't use my name!"

Powers played ignorant. "You ashamed of your name?"

"You know what I mean!"

The hounds made wild, mournful sounds that echoed and re-echoed through the hills, sounds that rolled and lifted and bounced and then died. Powers noticed that Mudd glanced hurriedly toward the barn. He then told Mudd that the old hostler was completely deaf.

"Why didn't you tell me that before?"

"Wanted to make you suffer."

Mudd said, "Talk sense. I'm not afraid. Here, now, here we are at the bunkhouse, and let's get to work. Sprinkle the kerosene along the side here, and then I'll light it."

"Inside!" Powers said.

Mudd stared at him, eyes strained. "Might be somebody sleeping in there," he croaked.

"What if there is? We'll kill him."

"You go — first."

Powers grabbed Mudd by the collar of his shirt. He twisted, and pushed Mudd ahead, the man gasping and lurching. Mudd slammed through the bunkhouse's door and fell to the floor inside.

"Who's home?" Powers demanded. There was no answer.

"Nobody here but us," Powers said, and he added: "Get to your feet, Mudd. Here, you sprinkle this kerosene."

Mudd lumbered up, said, "John, you had no call to treat me that way." Powers stood there, smelling the gloomy interior of the long room — the smell of dirty socks, of unwashed blankets, of shaving lotion and saddle leather. Then, with these smells came another — a sharp, alien smell that quickly permeated the room. The smell of kerosene.

Powers heard the gurgle of the kerosene leaving the can, and he heard the massive tread of Jacob Mudd, and the thought came: "How can a body so big know such great fear as he showed?"

Mudd's whisper was coarse. "I put it all over the bedding and on the wall. Now what do I do?"

"Light it afire!"

"It'll burn fast."

"We want it to burn fast."

Mudd lit the match. Through the dense darkness came the sudden stab of light, the flare of a match. Mudd's hands cupped this, and the flame showed his red flesh, and he moved over to a bunk, touching the burning match against the kerosene-soaked blankets. Flames showed the interior of the building clearly and the heat and smoke was gathering.

"We ought to break a window for air to come in so it could burn better."

"From the outside," Powers said.

"We got the thing on fire," Mudd said, and he sounded like a triumphant little boy. "We'll make that big Matt Williams sweat."

Mudd was out of the door when the rifle talked. The bullet hit into the side of the bunkhouse. Mudd hollered something, and he went down, and behind him John Powers, who swiftly raised his rifle. Powers shot and a man screamed in the haymow window of the barn.

Powers saw him clearly, for moonlight etched him. He realized he had scored a hit — the man had dropped his rifle. Through the roar he grunted, "That ol' hostler," and he shot again.

He saw the old fellow grab at the frame of the haymow opening, and he heard him scream. Then he saw the body falling, twisting as it came down, and he saw the man hit the ground, landing on his rifle.

The hounds were roaring behind the house — a wild canine cacophony of sound. Behind him suddenly there was a roar in the bunk-house and he turned; then tension left — some cartridges had exploded. He pulled at Mudd and said, "Where did he get you, Mudd?" and he got Mudd to his feet. The man's face was drained of blood, and his lips trembled.

"He — he didn't hit me —"

Powers said, "Oh, for Gawd's sake," and he slapped Mudd across the jowls.

"Come on, you fool!"

They walked across the clearing. Powers moved over to the body of the old hostler as he passed and he kicked the man in the head. Behind them the bunkhouse roared as flames took it. Rafters stood out, wrapped by flame; sparks flew with wild abandon; the wind moved against the burning building, giving it ventilation and draft.

Mudd went into saddle with swift alacrity. Powers turned his horse and the fire showed in the wild distended eyeballs of his bronc.

He finally caught Jacob Mudd's bronc.

He said, "You ride fast."

"A bullet comes fast," Mudd said.

Finally they gained a ridge. They breathed their broncs, and the only sounds were the rise and fall of horse-flanks, the creak of saddle leather. Behind them the flame kissed the Wyoming sky.

Jacob Mudd said, "What's next, John?"

"We join forces with Matt Williams."

Mudd peered at his partner. "Who," he asked the wide night, "is crazy now?" And he saw that Powers sported a secretive smile.

"We join forces with Matt Williams," Powers said. "We tell him about this tin, and this fortune here. Then we lead him against the nesters."

"Yeah?"

"We got to get rid of McKee and his Mexican. If we kill them, then the farmers will hightail out — those who are left alive."

"How about the squaw?"

Powers studied him, surprise showing. "What squaw?"

"This one of Big Bob's. Many Feathers, or whatever her name is."

"What makes you ask that question?"

"I don't like Indians," Jacob Mudd said. "Oh, well, forget it, and let's ride, Powers."

Mudd led the way, wide in his saddle.

Powers pondered on the man's words. Why had Mudd dragged the name of Many Feathers into this? She was only a dumb plodding squaw, and Matt Williams had kicked her out.

Powers gave up. He decided there was some things a man could never and would never understand.

They rode through the moonlight, heading for Powers' homestead. . . .

TWENTY

Buck McKee pulled his horse to a sliding halt and held up his hand as a signal for the farmers to rein in also. Beside him Tortilla Joe sent his bronc back on his haunches.

"You see somethin' ahead, Buck?"

Buck said, "Somebody on foot, comin' this way. Down in that little valley ahead of us, see?"

"I see heem now. He come on foot, like you say."

Betty's father, on his stirrups, gaunt and tall in the moonlight. "Lord, let it be my little girl. If them skunks has killed her —"

Buck hollered, "Betty!"

The figure stopped, stared up at them. Buck cupped his hands to his mouth and repeated his call.

Then, the echoes died; they waited. From the figure below came a weak cry. "This is Betty; this is Betty."

Her father spurred ahead, going down the

153

slope on sliding haunches, his bronc braced against the steepness of the slant. He rode like a man possessed with the devil. Behind him came Buck and Tortilla Joe, broncs braced on haunches, coming down with jarring jolts.

Behind them, dust lifting into the moonlight, rode the farmers. Rifles were held high, moonglow reflected from their steel barrels, and a grimness was with them — a grimness laden with danger and anger toward the Cross in a Circle cow outfit. Then Betty's father was beside her, holding her in his arms as she sat wearily on the grass.

Her father was praying, his lips close to her hair, and his words made Buck stop and take off his hat.

Buck knelt beside the tired girl. "What happened, Betty?"

With sobbing voice, she told about the nightriders. When she told about Sid Latham going down under lead she broke into wild weeping. And when her father spoke his voice was hollow and weak.

"They were betrothed, Mr. McKee. Only I knew it, for her mother would have objected, and she would have said she was too young to marry. They have met many times secretly, and I have known it. . . ."

Buck asked, "Who were they?"

She did not know. The night had hid them;

they had shot at her, too, but they had missed.

Her father said, in a croaking voice, "They — they shot at you, too? Shot at a girl?"

Rage was a living force in the eyes of Betty's father. Mike Latham swore with terrible frenzy.

"If they have killed my boy —"

Buck said, "Come on, men. Betty, stay with your father. He'll take you home." Buck waved his rifle over his head as a signal for them to follow him.

They streaked across the flat, and dust lifted; behind them, the farmers fell back. The Mexican rode like an immense jockey, high on his stirrups, his rump sticking out, and his head down low against the neck of his laboring horse.

"Matt Weeliams, he do thees," Tortilla hollered.

"Might have been Powers," Buck said. "He's got some dirty scheme up his dirty sleeve. He might be workin' both ends against the middle."

The Mexican shook his head with dogged insistence. "Thees time, Buck, I am the right, no? Powers he have only thees man Mudd weeth heem. Betty say many riders they burn down the shack."

"That's right," Buck said.

Suddenly, Buck pulled in his bronc. Riders

155

came around them, and dust was acrid and sharp.

"What is it, McKee?"

"What's ahead, Buck?"

Buck hollered, "Be quiet, men, and listen."

Some dismounted and held their broncs' noses to stifle loud breathing. Tortilla Joe went down and laid an ear against the earth. Then they heard the sounds. The wind took them to their ears.

"Horses," a farmer grunted. "Runnin' somewhere in the night. But from what direction do those hoof noises come, men?"

"From the direction of the Cross in a Circle," Tortilla Joe said. "Many riders too; they ride fast." He stood on his knees and said, "Look, hombres, at the Cross een the Circle. Fires!"

They looked in the direction of the Williams' ranch. There, arching against the sky, was the fire. It had long, red tongues that seemed to lick away the blackness of the night. Buck added all this together, coming to a rapid total.

"The Cross in a Circle has ride to fire Betty's father's shack. Then, while they were gone, somebody sneaked in an' set fire to their spread. Looks to me like the whole home ranch is on fire."

"Hope it roars up in smoke," a farmer

growled. "I hope the whul stinkin' outfit burns down to bare ashes, I do so help me!"

Tortilla Joe asked, "Any farmers not at the peecneec, mens?"

"We were all there," a man replied. "Why ask —" Then he got the implication of the Mexican's question. "If we were all at the gathering, then who set fire to the Williams' ranch?"

Buck said, "John Powers wasn't there."

One man crossed himself. "I do not like this idea," he intoned. "I am not one to fight fire with fire. I am a man of peace."

Buck said, "Come on, men."

Somebody had set fire to the Williams' ranch. The squaw Many Feathers hated Matt Williams, and she might have set fire to the Cross in a Circle outfit. Buck decided he would check with Sandra, who had stayed at the cabin with Many Feathers and young Paul Hammond.

The fair-haired girl had seemed to have a great interest in Hammond. Maybe that was because the farmer was down-and-out and wounded. But this was not the place, or the time, to think of Sandra. Accordingly he put her also out of his thoughts.

Mike Latham had ridden ahead, wild with haste, torn by fear for his son's safety. And when the others rode down on the burning cabin, the farmer was already there. He stood there, helpless against the heat of the ebbing flames, and when he turned his eyes, illuminated by the fierce fire, were bulging and flame-colored, and red hell was in the man's turbulent soul. "I can't find my son, McKee."

Buck gave the shack a quick appraisal. Within a few moments the fire would be burned down to the foundation. Already he could see the twisted frame of an iron bedstead in the ruins.

"The wind can't hit the fire here," a man said, "because of the hill behind the house. A few of us can stay close to keep it from spreadin' and the rest of us can search the brush."

Tortilla Joe said, "I help search, Buck."

Buck detailed two men to curb all attempts that the fire made to spread. They had buckets of water they had pulled from the pump and they stationed these at handy intervals. Buck and the others looked in the brush for young Latham. Buck figured that the search was useless.

Williams had burned down Jack Maloney's cabin, and the body of Maloney had been in the fire — a body riddled through with rifle and short-gun bullets. Such, he figured, would be the case with young Sid Latham.

Mike Latham was a madman, one moment

searching for his son, the next moment spewing curses at Matt Williams and his crew. Again and again the man demanded that the farmers band and ride for the Cross in a Circle. Buck was against this plan. He figured that Matt Williams wanted the farmers to do just this. Matt would then pick his own battleground; that would be a point in his favor; he could also ambush the farmers, for they were not experts at this rough-and-tumble form of fighting.

Men crashed through the brush, calling Sid Latham's name, ranging further and further out from the fire.

A man said, "His only kin. If the boy is dead in the fire it will kill him, McKee."

Buck waited, listening.

"Somebody hollered over that way," a man called.

That man had called falsely. Buck said, "Keep on searching," and they continued. Within an hour, the fire had burned down, and Tortilla Joe came and said, "Buck, where are you?"

"Over here."

Moonlight showed the soot-blackened wide face of the Mexican. "Buck, he ees een the fire. I can see hees body there."

"Be tough on his father."

Tortilla Joe crossed his massive bosom, his

stubby forefinger moving rapidly. "Eet ees the weel of God."

"I'll hate to see Mike Latham's face."

Already the word had reached Mike Latham. When Buck McKee and Tortilla Joe reached the site of the burned-out cabin, Mike Latham lay on the ground on his belly. His head buried in the dust, he sobbed broken-heartedly.

Farmers stood around occasionally glancing at the object in the ashes, then down at Mike Latham. Latham crawled to Buck and grabbed his pant leg and raised his face.

Buck looked down into a face suddenly old, suddenly aged. He looked down at eyes as burned-out as holes in a saddle blanket.

"McKee, this is not the job for one man. This is a job for all of us, for every man present."

Buck nodded, not trusting speech.

Again those cracked, trembling lips moved. "First, they killed Jack Maloney, a fine lad — my son's best friend. Then they shot Paul Hammond, and with God's help he will recover. Now my son is dead in there and his sweetheart is heart-broken."

Nobody spoke.

"McKee, we trust you. Powers called you and Mr. Tortilla Joe in because of your gun speed; he tricked you. McKee, lead us against

160

Matt Williams!"

Buck said nothing. Eyes were on him — probing, questioning eyes.

Mike Latham's voice was a cracked sound. "McKee, you and your partner know this brush fighting; we don't. Give me your answer, McKee."

Buck's eyes met those of Tortilla Joe, who nodded. Buck said, "On one condition, men."

"And what is that?"

"I am the boss — the complete boss. You obey me at all times."

"All right with me," a man said.

One by one, the farmers went by and shook hands with Buck McKee and Tortilla Joe, and thus, standing there beside the body of the burned youth, their agreement was made . . . and sealed.

TWENTY-ONE

Buck said, "Did you burn down the Williams' outfit, Many Feathers?"

She shook her head. "Me no burn it down."

"Then who did?"

She studied him patiently. She took her eyes from Buck and put them on Tortilla Joe.

"Woman out lookin' for you, Tortilla. She come from town on mule an' look for you. White woman."

Tortilla Joe spat on his hands, grinned, took a harder grip on his axe. "Margarita," he told the world in general. "She ees after me for the marriage."

Buck felt the raw rasp of impatience inside him.

"If you didn't burn the spread down, who did? I got reports that during the fire you were away from the Smith cabin. Where were you, woman?"

This was the second day after the fire had burned down most of the big Cross in a Circle

162

ranch. Buck and Tortilla Joe already had part of their log house up — in fact, they had the bottom tier of logs in place, about five logs high. They seemed in no rush to get it any higher.

"Me, I on trip."

"Where did you go?" Buck was persistent.

Sandra Smith listened. She had ridden to tell them that young Paul Hammond was sitting up. Buck had detected a bright happy glow in her dark eyes. He noticed, also, that she was not so interested in him. She had, in fact, almost ignored him, talking mostly to Tortilla Joe. And her talk centered around young Hammond.

Many Feathers looked at Sandra, eyes sharp behind their wrinkled lids. "You tell him I go from your cabin?"

"I had to. We're in this all together, Many Feathers. Buck is our leader and each of us has to work with him."

"Him good leader."

Tortilla Joe swung his axe with much vigor. "All the time there ees troubles weeth the womans," he grunted.

Sandra said, "Well, if that is the case, I'll go home then." She smiled at Buck, but her smile did not hold that old warmth. The girl mounted, riding sidesaddle, and rode away.

"Where were you?" Buck repeated.

163

Tortilla Joe leaned on his axe handle and watched, but said nothing. Back on the slope a cow bawled to her calf.

Many Feathers had not left them after she had ridden in the morning after the fire. She had never let the two get out of her sight. Just now, she seemed reluctant to talk.

"You ride over and burn down the Cross in a Circle?" Buck asked for the tenth time.

"This mans they call Mudd," she said, "he go around with a little hammer. He pound on rocks and look at them."

Buck had watched Mudd through field glasses. He had done some mental arithmetic, matching cause against effect, and he had come to the conclusion that John Powers and Jacob Mudd wanted Ringbone valley because of some mineral content. He did not know what this mineral was.

"He look for something, maybe?"

Buck pounded one hand against the other. "Many Feathers, did you or did you not set the Williams' spread on fire?"

"Why you want to know, McKees?"

Buck explained carefully. If she had not set the spread on fire, then somebody else had; if you were going to fight somebody, you had to know who your enemy was, and where he was located.

"I no light him," she said. "I no know who

burn him down."

Buck said, "That's all I want to know."

Tortilla Joe rubbed his whiskery chin. "Then who she ees burn the outerfeet, Buck?"

"Only two people, I figure. John Powers wasn't at the meeting. Neither was Jacob Mudd."

"We no know for the shore, Buck."

Buck and Tortilla Joe had, for some odd reason, placed a double row of logs for the base of the cabin. They had chopped out sections of these logs, placing one chopped-out area over the other. In this way, they had small windows out of which they could see. Sandra had openly doubted their sanity. Who, she had declared, would lie on his belly to look out a window.

The farmers were organized and ready to fight. Within the last few days, Buck and Tortilla Joe had organized them into a bunch of minutemen, ready to band together at a moment's notice.

Some of the farmers had wanted to ride against the Williams' spread, and that was just what Matt Williams had wanted them to do. With difficulty Buck convinced them it would be best that Williams moved against them, for a man always fought better on his own ground.

Buck's logic had been simple and in its simplicity lay its strength. By all tokens the Williams' gunmen would strike next at him and Tortilla Joe, for by now Williams knew that they were leaders of the farmers.

Each night saw a guard at each farmer's house. Back of that house on the hill, hidden in the brush, was a pile of loose wood, thoroughly soaked in kerosene. The minute the Cross in a Circle spread hit at any house the guard would light that pile of coal-oil soaked wood. Flame would instantly flare into the night. Other guards, stationed beside similar woodpiles, would instantly awaken the occupants of that particular house they guarded.

Thus, within a few moments, the entire valley would know whose property was being attacked, for on the hill behind that property the fire would be burning — a blazing tocsin summoning men to battle.

Also, a guard watched the Cross in a Circle.

The squaw started to move away. Then, she stopped, turned her bulk, and looked at Buck McKee with sharp eyes, then swung her gaze to Tortilla Joe.

"You my friends," she said, and she seemed to be talking to herself. "Years ago my people say this valley cursed with rich rock."

Buck waited, watching her.

"I make lie to you. I see Powers and fat

man ride for Cross in Circle. I want to kill Matt Williams, and I watch ranch."

"Yes," Buck said.

"Powers, him an' fat man — they burn the buildings. I see them in the night. They blame it on farmers."

Buck nodded. "Good deal for them, judgin' from their standpoint. So you saw this, eh?"

"I see that. They kill old man who shoot from the barn."

"I heard that the old hostler got murdered," Buck said.

Tortilla Joe spat, said, "Powers, he worse than Weeliams, Buck. He dirtier, I theenk."

But Many Feathers had more news to tell them. She had seen Powers and Jacob Mudd ride into the Cross in a Circle ranch the next morning. She had seen them talking with Matt Williams and Ag Keller. As the full implication of her words registered, Buck cursed with a wry anger rimming his words.

"Powers an' Williams has joined hands, Tortilla Joe. They've decided to work together, I'll bet."

"Maybe that ees eet."

Buck's eyes grew thoughtful. "I sure would like to know why Powers got the farmers in here, and just what is at stake in this trouble."

"So would I, Buck."

The squaw's eyes were shining beads of black obsidian.

"You got the right answers, eh?" Buck nodded.

Many Feathers waddled to her old horse. She led the nag over to a log, got on it, and laboriously mounted.

Finally, settled on the old crowbait, she spoke to Buck. "You hand me the rifle, Bucks?"

Buck handed her the old .30-30.

She had a knife in her belt — a long bladed affair in a buffalo-horn scabbard. She checked its security in the holster.

"I spy on Williams," she said, and her moccasins drummed on the old nag's bony ribs, getting him to a plodding walk.

The Mexican said, "Eef she meets Weeliams, she weel keel him, Buck."

"She'll sure try."

TWENTY-TWO

The air was thick with tobacco smoke. Men loafed in chairs, on the couch, and some lay on the floor.

Jacob Mudd sat with his back against the wall, gloomily studying John Powers, who sat on the floor across the living room of the Cross in a Circle ranch house. Mudd wanted to pull out and leave all this trouble behind. No metal — tin, gold, silver, lead — was worth a man's life, he figured.

Not more than ten feet away, was a raw-boned man of about fifty, who squatted and watched Mudd. He was Mudd's bodyguard. Jacob Mudd looked again at John Powers.

Powers got to his feet and walked outside. Out on the porch, another guard loafed; he saw Powers and he moved forward — a thin sallow gunman.

Powers looked into the dusk. "Moonlight and stars tonight," he said. The guard nodded.

Powers drew his lips down. "Where is Matt Williams?"

"He'll be back soon."

"I'll walk around."

The guard moved with him. Other guards watched. The place, Powers saw, was spiked with guards. He and Jacob Mudd were prisoners of Matt Williams.

He could see Williams' logic. He and Mudd had laid their cards face-up on the table and Williams didn't trust them any further than he could throw a bull-calf by his tail. That was good wisdom. Williams was afraid he and Jacob Mudd were double-crossing both the farmers and the Cross in a Circle outfit.

Williams undoubtedly figured he, Powers, could work both factions, keeping one posted on the other's doings or preparations. Then, when the time came for a surprise attack, there would be no surprise about it — the other side would be tipped off by Powers. And cowpunchers and farmers would fight to a finish, and, when the last shot was fired, Powers would be the winner. He would have eliminated each menace while he sat on the sidelines and cheered.

Williams was not chancing this.

Powers stopped at each burned building and stood and looked at the ashes. Dusk gathered. Impatience in him, Powers turned again towards the house, and then Matt Williams and Ag Keller rode into the yard.

They dismounted in front of him; neither spoke. Ag Keller finally said to the hostler, "Saddle me a fresh horse, fellow. That black stud of mine."

"Saddle my blue roan," Matt Williams said.

Powers said, "Well?"

Williams grinned. Hell was in his harsh eyes. "This is the night, Powers."

"We hit tonight?"

"We wipe them out . . . tonight."

Powers felt something grip his throat. He had long looked forward to this moment, and now that it had arrived he did not know just what to think.

Keller cut in with, "Matt, I'm goin' to the house an' git the boys ready, eh?"

"Do that, Keller bowlegged towards the porch. Powers asked, "We hit at McKee?"

Williams beat dust off his chaps with his hat. "No," he finally said. "We don't hit at McKee."

"Why not? He's the enemy. Get him an' his Mex an' these farmers'll run like scared cottontails."

Williams carefully recreased his hat. "McKee and the Mex have a fortress built, Powers. They act like they're building a house, but they ain't. They got about six logs high and about two deep. They aim to use it as a fort. They figure we'll hit at them, seeing they're the leaders."

"They are the leaders."

"But we don't hit there. We're not running against the enemy's hard spots, fellow. We're hittin' at another spot, savvy?"

"Where do we hit?"

But Matt Williams was heading for the house. John Powers watched him, blind rage in him; Williams had disregarded his question entirely. Powers felt a little helpless, and a lot more angry. Then logic came in and buried his anger under the cloak of discretion.

He followed the owner of the Cross in a Circle. Williams stopped on the steps, and he looked at the ruins of the burned-down buildings, and Powers saw the terrible driving hatred in his eyes. Williams would kill the man who did this. Mudd was weak. He might tell Matt Williams that he and Powers had burned down the Cross in a Circle buildings. Powers decided, then and there, to kill Mudd.

Under cloak of darkness, in the middle of the gunfight — Mudd would be killed. Powers made this decision, stored it in his mind, and moved behind Williams into the ranch house.

Williams said, "Up and in saddle, men."

They had horses ready and they lifted their

bodies into the dusk. Horses reared and pawed, and rifles sank into boots, their stocks protruding.

Williams waited, patient now, a dangerous man dangerous because of youthful ambition.

Jacob Mudd acted as though his legs were raw from riding, for slowly he settled himself in his kak. Powers and Williams saw this and their eyes met and Williams showed his smile only to Powers. Powers grinned. Neither man said anything. A guard rose close to Mudd. Williams held up his hand for silence.

Williams said, "There is no need for hurry. The moonlight will be with us within an hour. We ride in a body to the big cottonwood on the bend in Ringbone Crick. We stop there and I give each man his duty assignment. When we hit tonight we hit for the last time."

"We win," Keller said, "or we lose, eh, Matt?"

"That's it. Powers, ride beside me; I want to talk to you."

Powers rode close to Williams.

"Not McKee?" Powers asked.

Williams said, "We hit at Pete Smith."

Powers nodded. He saw the logic. He remembered Sandra Smith. He remembered her clean sweet beauty, and Powers seemed a thousand years old — he had no body nor thoughts nor morals nor hope. This feeling passed, and he said, "All right, we hit at Smith. But McKee and the Mex will horn in."

"I'll welcome that, Powers."

TWENTY-THREE

The scout rode a horse that had been run hard. The scout said, "They've left the Cross in a Circle. I seen them. This is it, McKee."

"Which way did they go?"

"I never watched them after they headed out. But they aim to hit at us farmers for sure, this time."

"Warn the rest of them," Buck said. "Then watch for the signal fire. You jest come from Smith's farm?"

"Jest come from there. So long."

The scout was gone.

"Thees ees eet, Buck. They heet at us."

"I doubt that."

"Why you say that, Buck?"

"Williams has had scouts out. They've seen us buildin' our shack. We got a fort here and they know it."

"They make examples of us, no?"

Buck said, "We'll wait and see, *amigo*."

They were squatting in the buckbrush on

the hill above their homestead. Moonlight was clear and below them was the fine line that was Ringbone Creek. Below them, too, was their fortress — a dark square in the moonlight.

"Where ees the squaw, Buck?"

Buck grunted. "Danged if I'd know. Haven't seen her since this afternoon. She's an odd old gal, eh?"

"Matt Weeliams," said the Mexican. "She wants to keel Matt."

Buck smiled. "Who doesn't?" He closed his eyes.

Suddenly a hand shook him. "Come awake, pardner, an' look! Over that way — toward Smeeth's home!"

Buck was on his feet. A fire was burning on the hill back of Pete Smith's farm. A signal fire, leaping toward the sky.

"Smith, eh, and Sandra is there — so is Paul Hammond."

Tortilla Joe ran for his bronc, tied in the brush. "We ride and meet the farmers, down along the creek, no?"

Buck was already mounting. "We meet there pronto," he gritted, and he loped out, horse digging dirt.

Over at the Jones's farm, the Jones boy saw the signal first. He came into the house. He was sixteen, big for his age; his eyes were wild.

"Dad, the fire — back of Smith's farm!"

"So the time has come, huh, son?"

"They're hitting Smith, Dad!"

Jones was an ex-schoolteacher — a thin, anaemic looking man of forty odd. He took his rifle from the corner. "Your rifle is over there son," he said quietly.

The boy said, "Right behind you, Dad."

Mrs. Jones caught her husband's arm. "I'm going with you, Dad."

"This is for the men, Rachel."

"I go too," the daughter said.

Mrs. Jones said, "When we married we said we would share and share alike, Verne. Somebody will die tonight because man is greedy. If it is you I want to be with you, and with my son."

"I want to be there too," the daughter said.

Jones said, "God is with the weak, and we are the weak. Death is a small item, for we all meet again in a Better Land. Get your pistols and we ride, family!"

The signal fire burned.

Buck and Tortilla Joe met the farmers at the appointed meeting-place.

Buck said, "I'm your leader. You appointed me yourselves. Therefore every word I say has to be obeyed."

"Amen," the minister intoned.

Quickly Buck outlined his plan of attack.

177

And they listened, and they nodded; they agreed. The men would fight in first, and behind them would come their women and the young folks. Smith and his family would desert their cabin and take to the timber, getting Hammond with them — they'd carry him, if needs be. Then the farmers would build a ring around the Cross in a Circle raiders, penning them in.

"Give us our stations," Jones said.

Quickly Buck designated the men who would attack from given points. Behind them the signal fire lifted, a glittering challenge to them.

"That is all," Buck said.

Tortilla Joe said, "There ees one theeng more, amigos. Our minister, he say a few words to Dios."

The Mexican's hat came down and was held over his barrel-like chest.

Other hats were doffed; heads sank down. And the minister prayed to God for aid, his voice clear and loud.

"Amen, brethren."

Buck said, "Thanks, brother," and then, "We ride and we ride fast. And good luck to you, our neighbors."

"The same to you, Buck."

Then they were riding, a body of riders, dark under the moon. Moonlight glistened on

178

upraised rifles; there was the smell of ageless dust; the good odor of sweaty horseflesh.

Buck swung his horse, and the riders went by. He saw men with old pistols, men with rifles; he saw women who, a few months before, had not known how to ride a horse. He saw the Jones girl, her dark hair in braids. He said, "Be careful, please."

The mother said, "Thank you, sir."

The girl looked at him.

"Mr. McKee," she said, "with you on our side, we will win."

Buck felt a moment of great reverence. Hoofs pounded, horses panted, and the fire burned, egging them on. His hand went out and met hers and held for a moment and he said, "Thank you for that, Miss Jones."

Her eyes glowed momentarily.

TWENTY-FOUR

It was the Crow squaw, Many Feathers, who brought the Ringbone Valley war to an end.

She saw Matt Williams ride out with his riders. She followed their progress, keeping to the rimrock ledges, riding the high dark lifts of the back country.

She followed them to the Smith farm.

The scout had already warned the Smiths, and they had taken to the brush. Sandra had lit the signal fire. Paul Hammond, prompted by the duress of the occassion, had left the cabin under his own power, although he was still weak.

Many Feathers sat her saddle for a while, building her plan of action; finally, rifle in hand, she slid from her old horse.

She would play a lone hand.

She saw Matt Williams dismount his riders, and they worked toward the Smith farm, moving through the brush. Pete Smith saw one of the Cross in a Circle riders, and he shot at him, and the battle started.

By this time, Matt Williams knew he was in for a fight. The signal fire, blazing on the hill, had told him that.

He said to Ag Keller, "Take the three men there and circle that butte and get Smith and put him out of business with a bullet."

"How about the girl?"

Matt Williams said, harshly, "Are you gettin' soft, fella? Kill her, of course!"

Ag Keller said, softly, "This is a rough deal. First, where is that squaw, and next this gent Mike Latham — he's wild about his son gettin' killed."

"We'll take care of both."

Matt Williams and Ag Keller had held a hurried consultation. The farmers would come in, and they would move back, and catch the farmers in a trap.

"That's it, Matt."

Accordingly, they had built a circle, then they moved back.

Many Feathers watched, face stolid. She had one job. She would accomplish that, or she would die. There had been only one man in her world. Big Bob Williams was dead. There would never be another man for her. She touched her swollen, ugly face. The boots of Big Bob's son had done that to her face.

Had Big Bob been alive, he would have

killed his son — his only son — for that.

Accordingly, the Crow squaw watched, and waited. She saw Buck McKee make his farmers dismount, and she saw the outline this battle was to take. She worked her way forward, moving swiftly despite her obesity, and her moccasins made little noise on the dried Wyoming earth.

Buck McKee had heard Pete Smith's shot, and had made his farmers dismount; they had moved ahead, rifles and pistols ready. The brush seemed to reach out and grab them. One moment they were in the open; the next they were out of sight.

Tortilla Joe worked at Buck's right, always out of sight, but always within hearing distance. The rifles and pistols were talking now, and their sounds were ugly in the night.

Buck stopped, stood in the dark shadows of a cottonwood. His spine was cold: he did not fancy this type of fighting. It was too secretive, too deadly, too unexpected.

Evidently some of the Cross in a Circle riders had put fire to Smith's cabin, for it burned with a sharp, blue flame that lighted the brush and the hills. It snarled and spat sparks upward, as though angry at man and his foolishness. Brands arched upward, landed, died.

Across the brush came the call, "Plows and harnesses," which was the signal the farmers had taken for recognition in the night.

The fight lasted about an hour. It was run and fire as you ran, shoot as fast as you could — hope to kill. Buck kept working his way around, looking for Matt Williams or Ag Keller. He had a plan and he hoped it would work.

He figured that if Matt Williams got killed or shot out of commission, the Cross in a Circle hands might surrender, being without a leader. If both Williams and Keller got put out of the fight, then he was sure the hirelings would drift out.

Before he met either, though, he downed one Cross in a Circle man. He did not kill the man but that was not his fault; he shot to kill. But he saw the man roll over, dropping his rifle.

Within thirty minutes, Tortilla Joe had a broken right arm. His hand was limp and blood ran down his forearm.

Tortilla Joe grinned good-naturedly, but it was a sickly grin — a tired, painful gesture. "Me, I theenk I sees the squaw a while backs, over there." He gestured with his pistol. "But I not sure, Bucks."

"Don't worry about her, Tortilla Joe. Get either Keller or Williams, and this is over."

Within ten minutes, Buck had shot down Ag Keller. Keller had darted across a small park and Buck had stepped out and called to him. Keller stopped, turned, said in a terrible voice, "McKee!", and his pistol had shown red. Buck shot him through the chest and knocked him down. Keller dropped his pistol, grunted, tried to get up, got to his knees and bent over.

Keller screamed, "Matt, I'm hit."

Matt Williams, who had watched from the brush, stepped out, his rifle on Buck.

Buck couldn't turn around fast enough to down Williams, for the Cross in a Circle owner had a gunsight on him. All Williams had to do was drop his trigger.

Buck had to raise his gun, turn, and then fire.

Matt Williams said, "This gives me pleasure, McKee."

Buck did not have to fire.

Williams was caving in, hand on his chest, his mouth open. His knees, too, were moving out from under him. His mouth was open and no sound came and that was odd. And then Buck realized the man was dead in his boots.

Ag Keller had rolled over on his side, and was out of this. Buck waited until the roar of the rifle rolled into oblivion and then he got to his feet.

"Tortilla," he said, "you got him."

But it was not Tortilla Joe who came out

of the brush. It was the Crow squaw, Many Feathers. She stood there, looking at Matt Williams' body, and her face was old, it was savage, it was gray with hate.

Buck said, "You — you killed him."

Her eyes were sunken and dead under the light of the moon. "I waited for this," she said.

Then, she turned, and went into the brush.

Behind Buck, a man threshed through buck-brush. Buck got to his feet and turned, then he lowered his pistol.

He said, "Williams is dead. Keller is wounded. Spread the word, quick."

Within ten minutes the Cross in a Circle gunmen were running. Within another five minutes, the farmers were alone — a jubilant bunch of men and women. Within another five minutes, Buck McKee and Tortilla Joe were riding out of Ringbone Valley.

The water was ice, coming from the mountain springs, and the man's heavy body knifed across it, as he swam overhand. He reached the far bank, sat on the grass, and said, "My arm, she ees well, Buck. She heal fast."

Buck McKee, naked as the day he had been born, lay on the rushes, looking at the blue sky.

"Good old Utah," he said. "One more day,

and we reach Marty's spread. Man, he'll run out, eyes sparklin'."

"I can sees heem now," Tortilla Joe said. "Buck, read the letter again to me, no?"

They lay on their naked backs and looked at the cloudless sky. The water was good. The earth was good. The sun was good.

"Sandra aims to marry Hammond," Buck said. "They'll make a nice couple." He glanced at his partner. "Better'n you an' Margarita."

"Margarita, she mad, Sandra say. Ag Keller, he talk, he go to jail. John Powers, he get keeled by Mike Latham.

"Jacob Mudd he talk like mad, Sandra write. There ees teen in the valley. Now there ees a big teen rush." He chuckled at that — a deep, heavy sound. "Me, I hear of gold rush, but never a teen rush."

"Tin, not teen."

Tortilla Joe said, "What the heck difference does she make — teen or tin? Let them struggle for eet. Buck, in my saddlebag, there are two *tortillas* — the last two fat Margarita she make for Tortilla Joe."

"What about them?"

"We eat them. We make toast with them."

"I don't like them. Why do we both have to eat them?"

Tortilla Joe waddled over and got the *tor-*

186

tillas and unwrapped them. Buck sat up and took one. "I'd rather have a beer," he grunted. "Whoever heard of eating a toast to somebody? You *drink* a toast, not *eat* one."

"We got no beer, so we eat a toast." Tortilla Joe's white teeth smashed into the *tortilla*. "To fat Margarita, who weel not marry me."

Buck bit, winced. "To Sandra," he said. "Sandra, with the pretty dark eyes. And to Ringbone Valley."

"And to Ringbone Valley," the fat Mexican intoned.

The employees of THORNDIKE PRESS hope you have enjoyed this Large Print book. All our Large Print books are designed for easy reading — and they're made to last.

Other Thorndike Large Print books are available at your library, through selected bookstores, or directly from us. Suggestions for books you would like to see in Large Print are always welcome.

For more information about current and upcoming titles, please call or mail your name and address to:

THORNDIKE PRESS
PO Box 159
Thorndike, Maine 04986
800/223-6121
207/948-2962